ISAAC ASIMOV

ROBOTS IN TIME

by
WILLIAM F. WU

THE LAWS OF ROBOTICS

1.
A robot may not injure a human being, or through inaction, allow a human being to come to harm.

2.
A robot must obey the orders given it by human beings except where such orders would conflict with the First Law.

3.
A robot must protect its own existence as long as such protection does not conflict with the First or Second Law.

Other AvoNova Books in
ISAAC ASIMOV'S ROBOTS IN TIME *Series*
by William F. Wu

PREDATOR
MARAUDER
WARRIOR
DICTATOR

Coming Soon

INVADER

ISAAC ASIMOV'S
ROBOTS IN TIME™

EMPEROR

WILLIAM F. WU

Databank by Matt Elson

A Byron Preiss Book

AVON BOOKS • NEW YORK

ISAAC ASIMOV'S ROBOTS IN TIME: EMPEROR is an original publication of Avon Books. This work has never before appeared in book form. This work is a novel. Any similarity to actual persons or events is purely coincidental.

An Isaac Asimov's Robot City book.

AVON BOOKS
A division of
The Hearst Corporation
1350 Avenue of the Americas
New York, New York 10019

This novel is dedicated to

The memory of my paternal grandfather,
Yuan San Wu,
who passed the story of the building
of the Great Wall to me
through my father

Special thanks are due during the time of writing this novel to Dr. William Q. Wu and Cecile F. Wu, my parents, for indulging my lifelong interest in history; Ricia Mainhardt; Robert L. DeCandido of the New York Public Library (Research) Preservation Division, for assistance with the descriptions of papermaking; and John Betancourt, Leigh Grossman, Keith R.A. DeCandido, and Byron Preiss.

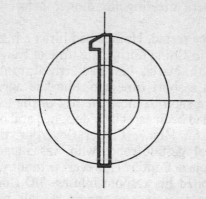

R. Hunter sat in the office chair of Mojave Center Governor, the robot he had been assigned to reassemble. Hunter had to decide what appearance to use on his next mission. He wore his usual northern European physiognomy now, with short blond hair and blue eyes. A brawny six feet six inches tall, he had been designed with the ability to change his shape and appearance at will and might have to do so for the next trip back into the past, to China in 1290.

First, however, he would discuss the question with the humans on his team. His internal clock told him the time was 6:49 P.M. They were having dinner now and would join him here soon.

After four previous missions into the past, Jane Maynard, the roboticist, and Steve Chang, the general assistant, had a routine established now. Since their return last night from the outskirts of Moscow in 1941, they had each had a good night's sleep. They had spent the day relaxing in Mojave Center, this new underground city in the Mojave Desert. Then Jane had called Hunter about an hour ago to say they were meeting for dinner before coming to see him.

While they rested, Hunter had hired a historian who specialized in China during the time of Kublai Khan to join the team. Marcia Lew had arrived from her home in Houston a short time ago. She had agreed to join Hunter here soon to meet the rest of the team.

Hunter had been especially designed and built to lead the search for Mojave Center Governor, the missing experimental gestalt robot who was supposed to be running Mojave Center. However, without warning, he had abandoned his responsibilities. MC Governor had divided into the six component gestalt humaniform robots out of which he was comprised and vanished.

Each gestalt robot had fled back in time to a different era. Hunter had led his team of humans on successful missions in pursuit of the first four component robots. Now they stood here in the office of MC Governor, merged and shut down, waiting for the last two in order to complete the Governor robot again.

"Hunter, city computer calling. The Governor Robot Oversight Committee is waiting for you on a conference call."

"Excellent. Please connect me."

The faces of the four Committee members appeared on Hunter's internal video screen in split portrait shots. As usual, they did not waste any time with social amenities. They exchanged greetings briefly, then Hunter got right to his report.

"MC 4 has been joined to the first three components who were already in custody," said Hunter.

"You're as efficient as ever," said Dr. Redfield, the tall blonde. She smiled approvingly. "You've progressed so quickly that I suppose it has been fairly easy for you."

"As I have said before, this does not predict the difficulty of the next challenge. I still cannot guarantee that the remainder of my work will be completed at the same speed."

"Where was MC 4?" Dr. Chin cocked her head to one side, looking at him with curiosity. "Nearby, this time?"

"In western Russia," said Hunter. He had not informed them of the time travel device and hoped that the necessity of doing so would not arise. He was deliberately vague in his reports. So far, his rapid success had satisfied them.

"We have very little to criticize." Professor Post stroked his black beard for a moment. "Nothing, in fact, that I can see. Where do you expect to go next?"

"I have a lead in East Asia," said Hunter.

"Really?" Dr. Chin said. "This is quite a change in geography."

"I have only preliminary information," Hunter said cautiously.

"Your information has always been good," said Dr. Khanna, speaking with his Hindi accent. "Your success could not have come about so quickly otherwise."

"I feel I must repeat that I can make no guarantee of my progress to come," said Hunter.

"Yes, yes," said Dr. Khanna impatiently. "You say that every time we speak with you. I will ask you the same question I posed last time. Do you have any reason to believe that the next mission will be more difficult than the previous ones?"

"I can only rephrase my original point," said Hunter. "I cannot predict the challenges that my team will face."

"We note your caution," said Dr. Chin. "And, as always, we wish you good luck."

"I'm satisfied, Hunter," said Dr. Redfield. "Maybe we should let you get on with your duties."

"I agree," said Hunter. "Do you have any more questions?"

No one did.

"Good luck," said Professor Post.

"Thank you. Good-bye." Hunter broke the connection. He could hear footsteps approaching the office door and recognized Steve's and Jane's patterns. "Come in," he called out, before they knocked.

Jane came in first, grinning. "Hi, Hunter." She shook her head, and her rich brown hair swayed. "Even after all the time we've spent together, you still surprise me sometimes. Was it our footsteps, our heartbeats, our voice patterns, or . . ." She shrugged. "I don't know what else."

"I recognized your footsteps," said Hunter.

Steve came in behind Jane. "Evening, Hunter."

"Good evening. How does your head wound feel?"

Steve grinned. "I wouldn't call it a wound, exactly. I still have a bump on my head, but that painkiller I got last night from R. Cushing took care of the headache."

"I contacted Cushing today, and he told me your medication will remain in effect for several days. At the end of that time, he expects you will be healed to a point where further medication is unnecessary. Do you feel well enough to join us for the mission to find MC 5?"

"Yes. I'll be fine. But I want to discuss whether you need me or not. Before the last mission, I wanted out because I didn't feel I was necessary."

"Oh, not again," said Jane. "We're a team. We don't have to talk you into going again, do we?"

"I'm not mad like I was last time," said Steve. "But I don't want to be taken for granted, either. Hunter, we know a nuclear explosion has eliminated Beijing, and you told us we're going to the time of Kublai Khan. I followed the news for a while myself this afternoon. But do you need me or not?"

"Yes, I believe so," said Hunter, as he heard the sound of footsteps approaching. "My concern is how to blend in with the local people as much as possible. I hired a historian named Marcia Lew who—"

"Right here," said a woman's voice.

Jane and Steve moved out of the way and Marcia came into the office. A young woman of Chinese descent, she wore a fashionable and precisely tailored black business suit. Her shoulder-length black hair was simply parted in the middle. She offered her hand to Jane and Steve in turn, as they introduced themselves.

"I apologize if I interrupted," said Marcia, in a precise and formal tone. "Hunter explained when we met earlier today that I'm the one who will need the most briefing, so he gave me a short introduction then about how Mojave Center Governor divided himself and how his components fled in time. I understand you two have already participated in four of these projects."

"That's right," said Steve.

"Hunter also told me that we are actually traveling in time, a concept that I have difficulty accepting. However, I have no choice but to believe all of you." She folded her arms and looked at Hunter.

No one spoke for a moment. Hunter saw that Steve was staring at Marcia in surprise. However, Hunter was not sure of the reason.

"Hunter, go on with your point," Jane said finally. "Explain why we need Steve. Then we can continue the rest of our briefing."

"We are going to China in A.D. 1290," said Hunter. "According to the historical data I took from the city library earlier today, we will be going to the city of Khanbaliq in a time of peace. Is this correct?" He glanced at Marcia.

"Yes."

"Hold it," said Steve. "Khan-what? Beijing is the city that just vanished under a mushroom cloud. Why aren't we going there?"

" 'Beijing' is the modern name for the same city," Marcia said primly. "A very old city on the same location called Yenjing was burned to the ground by Genghis Khan as he conquered northern China prior to the time we will visit. This is why no existing buildings in Beijing predate that time. When Kublai Khan ordered his new capital to be built just north of the remains, it was called 'Khanbaliq,' meaning 'city of the khan,' in Mongolian. When the Mongols were overthrown by the Ming Dynasty in 1368 that title no longer applied. It was renamed 'Beijing,' which means 'Northern Capital,' as opposed to 'Nanjing,' which is 'Southern Capital.' In fact, the modern city of Xian was once called 'Xijing,' or 'Western Capital' and—"

"*Okay*, okay, I get the point," said Steve. "It was just a simple question; I don't need a lecture on the subject, all right?"

"And the characters for Tokyo mean 'Eastern Capital,' " she finished calmly.

"Thank you," said Hunter, observing that Steve and Jane were glancing at each other. He could not read the exact meaning in their expressions. However, he understood that they were not happy with Marcia so far.

"You were discussing Steve's importance to the mission," Jane said.

"Steve, my concern is how to explain Jane's presence. You and Marcia, being of Chinese descent, will blend into the population just as Jane has done in our trips to seventeenth-century Jamaica, Roman Germany, and twentieth-century Russia. I must decide whether to maintain a European appearance or to alter myself to another look."

"So do you have a plan?" Jane asked.

"I will present a tentative one," said Hunter. "I understand that the capital of Kublai Khan in this time was a very international city."

"Correct," said Marcia. "Many Persians, Turks, Mongols, and other tribal nationalities were well represented. This is also the time of Marco Polo's presence in Khanbaliq, with his father and his uncle. In general, however, the international visitors will be from eastern and central Asia and possibly the Middle East. If you are thinking of European visitors, the Polo family may be the only ones."

"I propose that I maintain my European appearance and travel with Jane as a married couple."

"This would be acceptable," said Marcia. "If three members of the Polo family made the trip, one more pair of Europeans could have, too."

Hunter glanced at Steve for his reaction to the next part of this proposal. "I also suggest that Steve and Marcia present themselves as a similar couple, hosting us in what appears to be their country. The four of us would have a rationale for traveling together."

Steve glared at Hunter but said nothing.

Marcia glanced at Steve haughtily. "I suppose this makes sense. We have to fit into their society as smoothly as we can. I can tolerate some masquerading."

"Steve, do you agree this is logical?" Hunter asked.

"Yeah, I guess."

"We should present ourselves as visitors from a southern province," Marcia added. "This will explain any accent in our speech and unfamiliarity with details of Khanbaliq that never appeared in the history I have studied. We don't want to present ourselves as native to the city and then reveal our ignorance at the wrong moment."

"Which province do you suggest?" Hunter asked. "We should agree on one now."

"I recommend Guangdong, which is the southern-most province. We won't be likely to run into others from there who will expose us."

Steve nodded.

"And you must have some career, in case people ask what you do."

"Okay." Steve shrugged. "Like what?"

"A peasant or ordinary working man isn't likely to travel across the country in that time. I think you should be a scholar seeking a government appointment."

"Me? A scholar?" He grinned, glancing at Jane self-consciously.

"The top bureaucratic appointments in this time went to foreigners because Kublai Khan did not trust the Chinese. Many of the Turks and Persians I mentioned were in high government posts. Also, many of the established scholars refused to serve the Mongol government, even at the provincial and local levels. However, some young Chinese scholars managed to get into the lower ranks of the imperial offices. You're the right age."

"This sounds reasonable to me," said Hunter.

Steve sighed. "Okay."

"Marcia, I have much more to explain to you," said Hunter. "Time travel is the exciting part of the mission, but I must inform you of some background information. Have you been following the news today? Particularly, the explosion that destroyed Beijing? Millions of people died and China is in chaos, and has no government."

"The nuclear explosion? Of course. It's all over the news media right now. What does that have to do with a component robot in 1290?"

"The explosion was caused by MC 5. When the component robots reach the approximate time at which they fled back into the past, with a margin of error of several days, they explode with nuclear force."

"They do? Why?" Marcia's dark eyes widened with horror.

"Their atoms become unstable because of a problem they did not predict. They have miniaturized themselves to microscopic size with the same device that sent them back in time. This is what made them unstable."

"Why did they do that?"

"Apparently, they wanted to remain microscopic forever so they would not be involved with humans. They intended to avoid contact so they would not cause possible harm to people by changing the course of history."

"Of course. The First Law of Robotics says that 'A robot may not injure a human being, or through inaction, allow a human being to come to harm.' "

"That's right," said Jane.

"And I suppose if they were masquerading as humans, they would be in danger of being given instructions by humans that they would have to obey. As I recall, the Second Law of Robotics says, 'A robot must obey the orders given it by human beings except where such orders would conflict with the First Law.'"

"Show-off," muttered Steve, rolling his eyes. "All right, give us the third one, too. Get it over with."

Marcia arched one eyebrow at Steve and spoke in a monotone. "The Third Law of Robotics says, 'A robot must protect its own existence as long as such protection does not conflict with the First or Second Laws.' Now may we get on with this briefing, please?"

"The sooner the better," said Steve.

"I'm almost finished with this part," said Jane. "Marcia, the new problem is that the miniaturization turned out not to be permanent. The instability of that process has caused each component robot to return to full size at a different time in history."

"I believe I understand. At that point, of course, their interaction with humans becomes virtually inevitable." Marcia turned to Hunter. "Is this how you decide which period in history to visit?"

"Yes," said Hunter. "The site of the explosion in our own time reveals where to look. I made calculations from the records in the console of the time travel sphere that tell me when MC 5 was likely to return to his normal size. We must go back and try to apprehend him as soon as we can, before he influences anyone significantly. Returning him to our time with the time travel sphere will prevent him from exploding."

"I see," said Marcia.

"We're almost done with this background stuff," said

Steve. "Then we can head for the Bohung Institute. Tell her about Wayne, Hunter."

"Perhaps you can summarize that problem for us."

"I don't feel like it." Steve turned away from Marcia. "I'm just the hired hand, remember? I don't handle this theoretical stuff."

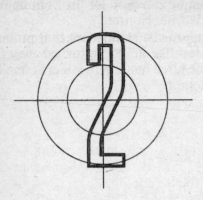

Steve could hardly believe that Hunter had hired someone as stuffy and pompous as Marcia. Though he felt bound by Hunter's genuine need for him on this mission, Steve already disliked Marcia more than any team member since he had first met Chad Mora, the paleontologist who had joined them on their first mission, back to the Late Cretaceous in the time of dinosaurs. Having to pretend he was married to her was going to make this trip even worse.

"I'll explain Wayne," Jane said quickly. "Dr. Wayne Nystrom invented the Governor robots, and he is angry that the Oversight Committee is leaving him out. He wants to get at least one of the component robots under his power so he can try to find out what went wrong himself."

"How does he intend to do that?" Marcia asked. "Is he trying to break in here or something?"

"No," said Jane. "Before Hunter got here, Wayne found the time travel sphere and has arranged to use it himself. He can apparently move through time without returning here. But on one occasion, he came back here and found a robot we had left here to apprehend him."

"What happened?" Marcia looked from Jane to Hunter. "You mean this robot didn't catch him?"

"No," said Jane. "We don't know exactly what happened, but we instructed the robot, R. Ishihara, to hold Wayne. We explained these instructions on the grounds that Wayne's actions in the past threaten harm to humans by changing history—the same concern we have over the component robots. That First Law imperative should have been sufficient to convince Ishihara to obey under the Second Law."

"Then why didn't it work?"

"I can only surmise," said Jane. "My best estimation is that Wayne somehow created doubt in Ishihara's mind that Wayne was causing a clear First Law imperative. That would eliminate the power of our Second Law instructions and allow Wayne to give him new ones."

"Robots are so logical and direct," said Marcia. "You really think this Wayne guy could talk Ishihara out of his direct orders?"

Jane shrugged. "He must have. After all, he's a roboticist; he's had plenty of experience with robot logic regarding the Three Laws."

"Wayne should be easy to spot. Marco Polo's family and Hunter and Jane may well be the only other Europeans in the capital."

"His family?" Steve reluctantly turned to Marcia. "I've heard of Marco Polo, but . . . was his family there?"

"He traveled to China with his father, Niccólo, and his uncle Matteo," said Marcia. "Marco will be, let's see, thirty-six years old in 1290. In 1292, he and his family started their trip back home to Venice."

"Hunter," said Steve, "can we get on with it? We won't find MC 5 by talking here."

"Yes. You probably saw the Security vehicle waiting outside. I will drive us to the Bohung Institute. But I must ask all three of you if you have received the vaccinations I arranged for you. And have you completed your sleep courses in spoken Chinese, Mongol, and Italian of this time?"

Steve and Jane both nodded.

"Yes," said Marcia. "I took the vaccinations a little while ago, and I arranged the sleep courses last night after I spoke to you from Houston. From your selection of Italian, I suppose you intend to meet the Polos?"

"I want to be ready for this eventuality," said Hunter. "I noticed in Marco Polo's book that he gives no indication that he ever learned Chinese."

"That's correct," said Marcia. "He seems to have managed for his entire seventeen years in China speaking Persian and Mongol, though I believe he must have picked up a few phrases of Chinese along the way."

"I would think so," said Jane. "But if Steve and Marcia are masquerading as southern Chinese, why did you want them to know Italian?"

"I want them to be able to understand what they may hear if we meet the Polos," said Hunter. "Obviously, Jane and I would do the talking in Italian. Now, I believe we are ready to go the Bohung Institute."

"Hunter, hold it," Steve said in confusion. "You're thinking of meeting Marco Polo? A guy who wrote a book? We could really change history if we influence him, couldn't we?"

"We must handle any meeting with the Polos carefully, of course," said Hunter. "Marcia, do you feel the danger of affecting Polo's book would be prohibitive?"

"No," Marcia said thoughtfully. "As long as we're careful, as you say. Frankly, he said just before he died that he had not told half the wonders that he had seen. For instance, he never mentioned the Great Wall, even though he lived close to it in Khanbaliq for many years. He probably saw the western end when he arrived from Europe and again when he went home. He never wrote about tea, though it had been a common drink in China for centuries."

"Good," said Hunter. "If we meet the Polos, we will simply exercise extreme care not to be worthy of appearing in his book."

"One more question, please," said Marcia. "Maybe the rest of you know this, but I don't. Why are we leaving at night, after a day's activity? Shouldn't we leave in the morning, when we're fresh?"

"We must arrive in the evening, when dusk will mask our sudden, unexplainable arrival from any potential witnesses," said Hunter. "We will therefore leave this evening, so that your schedules of sleeping and waking will match those of the society in which we will be a part."

"Where will we land?" Steve asked. "Out in the middle of nowhere again, I suppose."

"Yes—to avoid being seen by local humans," said Hunter. "Since I am unfamiliar with the exact details of the city, we must arrive in the countryside. This will minimize the chance of appearing right in front of people; if we do land near peasants, I hope the near-darkness will also disguise us. Our first task will be to find a safe place to sleep. In the morning, we will begin our search for MC 5."

Marcia nodded. "All right. I understand."

As the team left the office, Steve walked out last, wondering how much of a burden Marcia was going to be. By the end of the first mission, he and Chad had earned a mutual grudging respect. On the other hand, Rita Chavez, the historian on the second mission, had caused more problems than she'd solved. The other two, Gene Titus and Judy Taub, had been pleasant and reliable. However, tolerating Marcia's personality was going to be a trial.

Hunter drove the team through the clean, peaceful streets of the underground city. They were brightly lit, full of shops and restaurants. Hunter drove among both robot and human pedestrians, as well as other vehicles. The robots and humans who lived in Mojave Center pursued their daily routines, unaware of anything unusual happening in their midst. Steve wondered what they would think if they knew a device that could send humans and robots through time existed right in their city. Hunter had insisted on keeping their time travel a secret, however, and Steve had agreed that was a good idea.

When Hunter had first started his assignment in pursuit of Mojave Center Governor, he had arranged to shut down the Bohung Institute. A city Security detail guarded the exterior, and another robot, R. Daladier, had been assigned to replace Ishihara in Room F-12, where the sphere was located, in the unlikely event that Wayne Nystrom appeared there. When the team entered Room F-12, Steve saw that Hunter had already prepared their clothing and money for the trip.

"I had two sets of clothing made today," said Hunter. "I was not certain if we would masquerade as people of some wealth or not, so I prepared one set to imply wealth and one to convey modest means. Also, I have provided two outfits in each set, so we will have a change of clothes with us. Marcia, please check them for authenticity. I can assure you that no synthetics have been used, of course. You will each have a radio communicator in the form of a lapel pin, as before."

"We should wear the better clothing," said Marcia briskly, glancing at the two stacks.

Steve watched as Marcia walked over to the stack of neatly folded black and gray silk. She lifted a long black robe and held it out at arm's length. The robe was shaped in a rough triangle, flared at the bottom with a neck that simply overlapped, like a bathrobe. From its size, Steve could see that this was for Hunter.

"This is fine," said Marcia, folding it again.

"What about the neck?" Steve asked. "In all the old pictures I've seen—and the movies set in pre-industrial China—the gowns had these tight collars that stand straight up around the person's neck."

"They're called Mandarin collars," said Marcia, as she set Hunter's gown aside and shook out a pair of baggy trousers. "They came into style many centuries later." She glanced over the trousers, turning them in her hands. "Your research has served us well." She set those down and picked up an identical set of clothes in Steve's size. "If these are in the same style, I don't need to examine them."

"They are identical except for size," said Hunter. "Will wearing identical colors be acceptable? The social acceptability of this was not mentioned in the history I found. Also, embroidery was available but I felt we should appear to be moderately successful rather than very wealthy. So I chose clothing in solid colors."

"I agree," said Marcia. "Appearing modestly well-to-do is wise. It will fit the roles of merchant and aspiring scholar that we have chosen. Further, black is good, a sign of prosperity. Since the number of dyes was limited in the society we will visit, most people in a given economic level wore fairly similar clothes."

"What about ours?" Jane pointed to the pile of gray clothes.

"They should be similar." Marcia lifted a plain dark blue robe and then a matching pair of loose trousers. "Yes, these are fine."

"Similar?" Steve shook his head. "The cut is exactly the same, isn't it?"

"Yes," said Hunter. "The styles were very loose. No form-fitting was involved."

"These are fine," said Marcia. "But I don't see any coats. What time of year are we going to visit?"

"Late summer," said Hunter. "It would be August according to our calendar, though of the course the Chinese are using their lunar calendar."

"Khanbaliq is pretty far north. The nights could be chilly even in summer."

"My data shows that fur coats would be commonly used in cold weather," said Hunter. "This is a problem we faced on an earlier mission. We do not use real fur in our time and I dare not take artificial fur back with us. So if we need coats, we must buy them there." Hunter pointed to a small pile of coins. "I have gathered authentic coins from that time for us to use, as we have on earlier missions."

Marcia picked up a coin and looked at it, nodding. "Paper currency was in use during this time. I should think it would be easy to imitate."

"I did not attempt to locate any surviving bills to use as models. The likelihood of their surviving to our time was too low."

"I'm going to change," Steve said impatiently, picking up his clothes and heading for the adjacent room.

"You do not have your shoes," said Hunter. "Or the under robe."

"Huh?" Steve stopped and turned around again, looking at Marcia.

She picked up a pair of shoes from the counter. As she turned them over in her hands, all Steve could see was flimsy black cloth over flat, heelless soles. She held them out to him.

"Those are shoes? What are they made of?" Steve asked doubtfully, as he took them from her.

"The soles are woven hemp," said Hunter. "The rest of each shoe is just cloth."

"That is an authentic design," said Marcia.

"However, under pressure from the First Law, I arranged for the inside of the shoes to have some arched shaping and padding for your feet," Hunter added. "This is an improvement that I must hope does not influence anyone in the past, but I believe the likelihood of anyone noticing the inside of our shoes is very small."

"Fine with me. I just want to get on with it." Steve also accepted a plain white under robe from Marcia, and went to change in the adjoining room.

The robes and trousers felt more uncomfortable than the clothing Steve had worn on earlier missions. The baggy trousers and flowing robe, even after he had tied the sash, felt weird. The shoes fit all right, at least. He rejoined the others with a self-conscious scowl.

Jane glanced at him and took her turn without saying anything. Marcia took no notice of him, instead looking closely at each coin. Hunter gave Steve a cloth bag containing the change of clothes for everyone.

Steve waited in silence. He hoped that this mission would end more easily than the others. Between Marcia's arrogance and these bulky, uncomfortable clothes, he did not expect to enjoy this one very much.

When they had all changed clothes, Hunter opened the big sphere and helped them inside. He took a moment to set the console and then joined them. When he closed the sphere, they all slid together in the darkness, jumbled in the curved bottom.

A moment later, Steve tumbled to the ground among some green plants. The air felt cool but not uncomfortable. To his right, the sun was low over the horizon. Hunter, Jane, and Marcia had landed right next to him.

They were sitting up on fairly level ground in some sort of cultivated field. Steve did not recognize the tall green stalks around them, which blocked their visibility beyond a few meters. He pushed himself up to a sitting position.

"Is anyone hurt?" Hunter asked.

"I'm fine," said Marcia.

"Me, too," said Jane.

"I'm okay," said Steve, getting to his feet and pulling his robe straight. Now he could see over the stalks around him. "But we don't have much daylight left. Where are we going from here, Hunter?"

Hunter stood up and pointed to the west. The glare of the sun nearly hid the sight of some high walls and towers in that direction. "That is Khanbaliq."

"Let's get going," said Steve, hoisting the cloth bag. He pushed his way through some of the stalks. "Anybody know what this stuff is?"

"Chinese sorghum," said Marcia, glancing at it as she stood and adjusted her own robe. "It's a common crop here, and closely related to the western variety."

Now that Steve was standing, he could see people walking toward the city on a nearby road. "We're lucky we landed in this field, Hunter. Otherwise, we would have landed in plain sight of those people." A dry breeze blew dust along the ground.

"That's true," said Jane, brushing dust off her robe. "If they see us walking out of the sorghum field, I hope they don't ask us what we were doing here."

"Lodging for the night is a bigger worry," said Hunter, pushing his way forward through the plants. "Steve is right. We must walk."

"Is it always so dusty?" Jane asked.

"Yes," said Marcia. "The soil is called loess, comprised of deep layers of dust brought here by prevailing easterly winds from the west."

Rolling his eyes impatiently, Steve gestured for Jane and Marcia to follow Hunter. As usual, Steve went last. Gradually, they picked their way through the stalks and reached the dirt road.

Poorly dressed, barefoot peasants were leaving the city. Some rode empty carts pulled by ponies or donkeys. Others led their work animals on ropes at a walk because their carts still contained some unsold produce.

Other people, better dressed, walked or rode on the way into the city. Many of them stared at Hunter and Jane in astonishment. The remainder plodded past without noticing them, perhaps too weary to look up.

Steve strode up next to Jane as the team began walking on the road toward Khanbaliq. "I can see that the people leaving town are farmers. But who are all these people going into the city with us?"

"I don't know." Jane turned to Marcia. "Is this a normal day, do you think? Or is something special happening?"

"In this time of peace and relative prosperity, I would say this is a normal day. I believe the people heading back into the city are merchants and maybe even scholars. They either have arrived from other cities the way we will claim to have done, or else they made day trips to nearby villages."

"Commuters, you mean." Steve grinned.

"Well—yes," she said stiffly.

Steve laughed, not at his little joke but at the fact that Marcia didn't even seem to recognize it as a joke. Jane elbowed him, scowling. Steve shook his head, openly showing his amusement.

"Marcia, do you expect we will have any problem finding lodging?" Hunter asked. "If the city has many visitors, they may have filled the inns already."

"I don't expect a problem," said Marcia.

Hunter turned to Jane. "Do you have any thoughts about where we should begin searching for MC 5?"

"Well, MC 5 specialized in the administration of Mojave Center. I think he will almost certainly be drawn to the heart of the government."

"In this society, that is ultimately the Emperor himself," said Marcia.

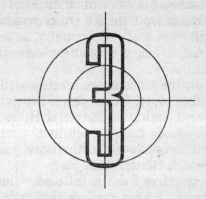

The team walked in silence as they slowly drew closer to the towering walls of Khanbaliq. The sun sank lower in the west beyond the massive walls. Steve was glad he did not have to listen to another lecture from Marcia.

As the team approached the city gate, Steve saw several guards impatiently waiting for sundown, when they could close the gate for the night. They wore full armor and sword belts, and each had a spear in one hand. As they leaned on their spears, they talked quietly to each other.

"Maybe the guards can direct us," said Hunter.

"Possibly so," said Marcia.

"I wouldn't ask them," Steve said quickly. "Guys in a job like that are trained to be suspicious of people from outside. At least, wait till we're inside and then ask them."

"Very well," said Hunter. "However, I see that they are not questioning anyone. Everyone simply walks through."

"They don't have modern immigration problems at a city gate in this time," said Marcia. "In times of war, they watch out for the enemy, of course, and sometimes in peace they are concerned with bandits. In this time, however, the country is really secure. The city wall is just a precaution against trouble in the future."

No one on the team spoke as they walked through the gate. Steve avoided the eyes of the guards, who in any case were staring at Jane and Hunter. Once the team passed inside the gate without incident, Hunter stopped and turned to a short, stocky guard who had turned to watch Hunter walk past.

"We are travelers from a far land," Hunter said in a formal tone. "Where can we find lodging in your city?"

The guard stiffened in surprise at being addressed. "Oh, uh . . ."

His partner, a slightly taller, slender man, stepped forward. "Many foreign visitors live near each other in one neighborhood. Is this where you would like to go?"

"We would," said Hunter. "Where can we find this neighborhood?"

"It is near the palace," said the guard, pointing. "Eight blocks east along this avenue, then turn to your right. I might suggest the Inn of the White Swan." He grinned ingratiatingly. "You might tell them the guards at the west gate sent you."

"Thank you." Hunter turned, gesturing for his team to follow. He led the way up the avenue in silence until they were out of the hearing of the guards. "Marcia, is this information consistent with yours?"

"Yes. Many of the foreigners here live near the palace so they can attempt to get audiences with either the Emperor or important ministers."

Steve looked up and down the streets as they walked. Despite the growing darkness people remained out everywhere. Merchants were lighting candles inside paper lanterns hanging from poles to light their shops.

"The shops are staying open, aren't they?" Steve asked. "Is that normal?"

"In the summer, yes," said Marcia. "People like being out in the evening when it's cool, so the merchants try to attract their business then."

"And all these streets are laid out on a right-angle grid," said Jane. "It looks very modern. I guess I expected narrow, twisted streets going every which way."

"Cities of that sort grew spontaneously," said Marcia, in her formal tone. "Khanbaliq was a planned city, laid out from the beginning as Kublai Khan's capital."

"Was it the first?" Jane asked. "As an example of urban planning, I mean."

"No. I don't know which city in the world has that honor." Marcia shook her head. "I know that in China, the Tang Dynasty capital of Changan was built during Europe's Dark Ages on a right-angle grid."

The team walked in silence for a while, looking at the sights. Other people continued to stare at Hunter in particular, whose height remained visible by his silhouette even as the shadows deepened. In the growing darkness, Jane's facial features and brown hair were no longer obvious.

"It looks . . . well . . . normal," said Steve, after a while. "We haven't been to a place like this before."

"That is true," said Hunter. "The buccaneers dominated the docks of Port Royal. Moscow in 1941 faced a foreign invasion. Our other missions did not take us to cities at all. This city has a normal, functioning society at this time."

"Most of Asia was—is, rather—at peace now," said Marcia. "The Mongols ruled only part of the Indian subcontinent, and did not rule Japan or the jungles of southeast Asia, but khans ruled the rest of Asia. Nominally, they all recognized Kublai Khan as their overlord."

"Wow," said Jane.

Steve clenched his teeth. He could hear another lecture from Marcia starting.

"Kublai Khan attempted two invasions of Japan, both of which failed," Marcia added. "One fleet was destroyed by the divine wind the Japanese call the original 'kamikaze.' And Mongols did conquer and rule part of northern India."

"They did?" Jane looked at her.

"The word 'Mogul' is a corruption of 'Mongol,' " said Marcia, "from India."

"Hunter, we must be getting close to the area," said Steve. He was hoping to stop Marcia by changing the subject.

"We have only passed four blocks," said Hunter. "That is not far enough."

"Well, tell me, where are we going to stay? Another inn, I suppose? You want to look for the one the guard mentioned?"

"That would be acceptable," said Hunter. "As you have said to me at certain times, we must improvise."

"It looks safe," said Jane. "In Port Royal, I always felt that any buccaneer could be a thief or a cutthroat. Here I see lots of young women walking around casually by themselves."

"It's a prosperous, peaceful country," said Marcia. "One that is ruled by an Emperor with absolute power. In fact, a historian once said that in Kublai Khan's time, a young woman could travel alone from Palestine to Korea with a sack of gold and not be bothered by anyone."

"Hard to believe," Steve muttered. "That is, without robots around."

"The death penalty was used freely," said Marcia.

"We must all remember that," said Hunter.

"But I wonder what MC 5 will try to do in a society that is fundamentally safe for humans," said Steve.

"I would not characterize it as safe," said Hunter, "not when the death penalty is utilized frequently."

"I think that kind of concern might provide our answer," said Jane. "That is, MC 5 may try to change government values and policy. I suppose that would mean influencing Kublai Khan himself. Marcia, what do you think?"

"Well, you're the roboticist, of course," Marcia said carefully. "I don't know how this robot thinks. But in terms of the way this society operates, your idea makes sense. At the very least, someone who wants to influence policy would try to become involved with the circle of advisors around the Emperor, maybe by working for one of them."

"How would MC 5—or anyone else—go about accomplishing that?" Hunter asked.

"Through connections," said Marcia. "Introductions are very important here."

"We know he doesn't know anyone here," Steve said impatiently. "He's going to show up naked, like the other component robots have. Long before he gets a job with the Emperor, he'll have to find a pair of pants."

Jane laughed. "That's true, but the others all managed. MC 5 will too, I'm sure."

Steve shrugged. "I think we'll find him out on the

street somewhere, not in the halls of government." He looked up the street. "We must be getting close to this neighborhood by now, Hunter."

"We will turn right at the next block," said Hunter. "Marcia, how would MC 5 create the kind of network he needs in this society when he arrives here without contacts of any kind?"

"Well . . . what kind of education does he have?"

"Education?" Steve snickered. "What does that have to do with what a fleeing robot does?"

"Has he heard of Marco Polo?" Marcia asked pointedly. "If so, he might begin with him."

"I do not know exactly what data the component robots have," said Hunter. "However, I think MC 5 could very likely have at least a passing knowledge of Marco Polo. How would MC 5 make use of this information?"

Marcia glanced at Jane. "Is that a robotics question? Or a historical one?"

Jane shrugged, smiling. "Hard to say. You start."

"Well, during this time, Marco Polo—as opposed to his father and uncle, who were advanced in years now— has been a traveling envoy of the Emperor, visiting various Chinese provinces and returning to report to Kublai Khan. Right now, he is back in Khanbaliq."

"So he could be found," said Jane.

"Yes. And he's respected at court, a familiar name and face to many people. I think MC 5 could track him down without great difficulty."

"Then so can we," said Hunter. "We shall begin tomorrow."

Hunter led them around a corner and up a smaller street. By this time, night had fallen completely, but the moon was nearly full. It shed a great deal of light out of the cloudless sky. Around them, hanging paper lanterns lit all the little shops lining the street.

"This isn't a residential block, Hunter," said Steve. "Maybe we should ask for directions again."

"Steve should do it," said Marcia. "Ask one of these merchants. But I don't recommend that Inn of the White Swan. The guards probably get a kickback for mentioning it, and we'll have to pay a higher rate to cover it."

That was a principle Steve understood. Wearily moving the cloth bag to his opposite shoulder, Steve walked up to a shop that had no customers. A young man behind the wooden counter was wiping it off perfunctorily with a damp cloth. A woman sat on a stool, yawning, with a sleeping baby in one arm. Two older children were scrubbing out a large iron pot.

"Good evening," Steve said politely. "We are travelers from outside the city. Can you tell me where we might find lodging for the night?"

The man's face tightened with annoyance. "You don't want anything to eat?"

Steve pulled a couple of small coins out and laid them on the counter. "We may be here for some time, friend. Tomorrow, we'll be hungry all over again."

The other man forced an affected smile. "Of course, of course." He scooped up the coins without looking down at them. "I am Liu Guan, at your service. May I suggest the Prosperity Inn, two blocks south on your left?"

"Thank you." Steve returned to the others and pointed down the street. They all started walking again.

"You had to bribe him," Jane asked, "just to answer a question?"

"Yeah."

"Well, that label is a little harsh," said Marcia. "Call it a tip."

Steve said nothing, afraid he would start Marcia on another boring lecture. Instead, he walked faster, looking into the shadows ahead for the Prosperity Inn. The others did not speak, either. He hoped Jane and Hunter were also learning that inviting Marcia to talk was a bad idea.

Soon a large, single-story building came into view with a long, vertical sign running down the left side of the entrance. In the yellowish light from the lanterns hanging from the eaves, Steve could read, PROSPERITY INN. Similar light illuminated the shades on the windows.

"Which one of us should make the arrangements?" Hunter asked Marcia.

"Steve," said Marcia. "You and Jane are masquerading as foreigners, and in this society—and as Steve's wife—I would not take that kind of initiative while he's here. But we'll all go in together."

"Okay," said Steve. He led them inside.

Small flames burned in brass oil lamps resting on wooden tables, lighting the room. A portly man with gray hair hurried forward to greet them. He wore a light blue robe similar to Steve's.

"Welcome, friends. Welcome." He bowed at the waist.

Remembering Marcia's briefing on the subject earlier, Steve imitated the man's bow.

"You are together? Two families?" The innkeeper looked in surprise at Jane and Hunter but said nothing else.

"Yes," said Steve. "My wife and I are hosting two guests from another country. I am a scholar seeking an appointment."

"Ah!" The innkeeper nodded eagerly. "Perhaps you would like a private bungalow, then? We have several in the courtyard behind the main building for special guests. I can offer you a bungalow with two bedrooms."

Steve glanced back at Hunter, who nodded.

"How much?"

"One silver per night."

Steve had no idea if that was a fair price or not, but he suspected the innkeeper assumed he would bargain. Casually, he glanced back at Marcia, who shook her head slightly. She stroked her hair with two fingers and wiggled them a little.

"Too high," Steve said firmly to the innkeeper. "Two." He had no idea what this meant, but it was the best he could do without revealing his ignorance.

"Two—coppers?" The innkeeper folded his arms. "No. Six coppers."

Now Steve knew where he stood. "Two coppers," he said confidently.

"Hm, well, maybe five. This is an entire private bungalow, you know."

"Two."

The innkeeper hesitated, glancing at all of them. "Four coppers."

"Two."

"No. Four."

Steve turned and walked back toward the door, grinning when he had his back to the innkeeper. "Come on." Without looking behind him, Steve opened the door and walked back outside. The sound of footsteps told him that the rest of the team was following him without speaking. Then, as he expected, another set of footsteps ran after them.

"Fine, fine. Two coppers a night for my special guests," the innkeeper called.

Steve stopped and looked back. The innkeeper smiled eagerly, gesturing for them to return. The team members waited for Steve's reaction.

"Two coppers," the innkeeper repeated.

"Fine," Steve echoed. "We will stay."

The innkeeper led them through the main building and out a rear door. It opened on a courtyard enclosed on all four sides by a high masonry wall. Several bungalows stood lined up in the courtyard; in the shadows, Steve could not see how many. Carrying a small brass oil lamp, the innkeeper led them to the first bungalow. He lit the hanging lamps over the door and then two more small brass lamps inside.

Steve glanced around inside. It was clean and nicely furnished. The tables and chairs were made of plain but highly polished wood, intricately carved in patterns with tight curls. The innkeeper led them to both bedrooms; the heavy bed frames were made of the same kind of wood, and quilted cotton comforters covered them. A small fireplace, which they would not need, warmed the bungalow in winter.

"It is adequate." Steve tried to sound unenthusiastic, to maintain his bargaining position in the future.

Hunter paid the innkeeper without speaking.

The innkeeper walked backward out of the door, bowing to them repeatedly, and closed it behind him.

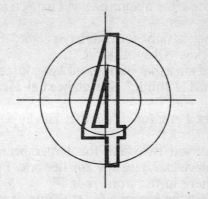

Steve let out a breath of relief and grinned at the others. "I'm glad my bargaining worked out. I didn't know what I was doing."

"You got my signal," said Marcia. "Very good. When we know the proper price of goods and services, bargaining is easy enough."

"We aren't cheating him, are we?" Jane asked. "We're only paying a small fraction of what he wanted."

"No," said Marcia. "He wouldn't have accepted if he could get a better price from someone else. It's late now and this bungalow would probably go empty tonight without us. Besides, the economy isn't strong here right now."

"Huh?" Steve was surprised. "I thought Kublai Khan was some kind of great benevolent dictator."

"For his time, he was very enlightened," said Marcia. "But the Mongol emperors were not good rulers economically. The first issue of paper money from Kublai Khan, made in 1260, was recalled three years ago in 1287, on a one-to-five basis—your money was only worth twenty percent of its face value. Another depreciation of the same magnitude will happen again in less than twenty years—"

"So money is tight for ordinary people," Steve interrupted quickly. "Okay, I get it."

"I'm tired after that walk," said Jane, just as fast. "I'm ready for bed, I think." She glanced at Marcia warily. "How about you?"

"Well, yes, I am, too. It's rather late by our schedule, isn't it?"

I suggest you two take the larger bedroom," said Hunter. "Steve can have the smaller one. I shall spend the night here in the front room."

"Always on the lookout for the unforeseen danger." Steve grinned. He took his change of clothes for the morning out of the bag, then handed the bag to Jane. "Well, I'm ready for a good night's sleep, too. Good night."

Dr. Wayne Nystrom landed flat on his back at dusk on the edge of some plowed field. The ground and air temperature were warm; this felt like a summer evening, which was what he expected. Next to him, he could see R. Ishihara sitting up. They both wore the tunics, leggings, and boots that Ishihara had originally designed for their trip to Roman Germany in A.D. 9. Wayne also still wore a long fur cloak that he had acquired, though Ishihara had traded his cloak away on their most recent trip to the area around Moscow in December 1941.

Wayne pushed himself up into a sitting position and saw a group of ten or twelve people standing about ten meters away, staring at them in shock. They wore thin shirts and trousers, and carried hoes, rakes, and scythes over their shoulders. Their faces were shadowed by basketlike hats made of woven grass.

With a sudden chorus of frightened shouts, the entire group turned and ran.

Wayne glanced around in other directions. Only a few meters away, an unpaved road led to a city that was visible in the distance. Many people were on it, going both to and from the city. "What do we do now? They saw us appear like magic."

"I do not know," said Ishihara, as he stood up. "Have we arrived in the right location? If not, we can simply move in time again and hope that seeing us arrive will have no serious effect on them."

"This looks like the right place," said Wayne, getting to his feet. "At least, I'd say that group is a bunch of Chinese peasants. And the weather feels right."

"I agree."

"The measurements I took from the console on the time travel sphere indicated that I should set the controls for the outskirts of Beijing in 1290," said Wayne. "If that city's Beijing, then this is where we want to be."

"The system has always worked correctly before," said Ishihara. "Apparently it is still reliable."

Wayne looked down the road. The peasants had stopped running. Now they were talking excitedly among themselves, while still watching Wayne and Ishihara suspiciously. "I don't know what kind of explanation we can give them. Maybe we better start walking."

"Set the belt unit for another time," said Ishihara. "If we have to use it in hurry, it will be ready."

"Yeah." Wayne paused and set the unit for the same location three hours later, after dark. Most likely, no one would be out here then. He glanced back at the group of peasants and froze.

They were coming closer, slowly. The men who held long-handled farm implements advanced in the front, holding their tools forward as weapons. Other men and women, holding smaller tools, followed them. Some were shouting angrily.

"Be prepared to trigger the belt unit," said Ishihara. "It is too late to run from them."

"All right. But maybe we can communicate somehow. I don't suppose you know any medieval Chinese, though, huh?"

"No, I do not."

Wayne forced a smile and held up a hand in greeting. "Hello," he called out. More softly, he added, "I'm hoping they can understand a friendly tone of voice."

The peasants stopped, still speaking excitedly among themselves. They kept their tools high, however. None of them looked away.

"I strongly recommend you trigger the belt unit," said Ishihara.

"They keep saying something like *'guei'* or *'kuai'*— something like that," said Wayne. "Any idea what it means?"

"No," said Ishihara. "And I must remind you that the First Law will force me to take the belt unit away from you and trigger it myself if they come much closer to us."

"Well, they stopped when I smiled at them just now and said hello. Maybe we can get through to them. Show them that both your hands are empty. And smile." Wayne felt more frightened than he sounded.

Ishihara held both his hands out, open, and smiled. "I think this word they keep saying means something negative, from their tone of voice. They fear we are a couple of *gueis*."

"Whatever they are."

"Yes."

"The word must mean some kind of supernatural creature—you know, a demon or a fairy or something else that can appear magically."

"It must mean an evil creature of some type," said Ishihara. "They would not be as afraid or as hostile toward a good spirit. I surmise that our European appearance has also increased their fear to some degree. Certainly these ancient German tunics and cloak make us look barbaric."

"Hey! Maybe we can use this. We're good spirits. We have to tell them we're good spirits."

"This will be a difficult distinction to make without a language in common," said Ishihara.

The peasants had begun approaching them slowly once again.

"No *guei*, no *guei*." Wayne forced himself to smile even more broadly than before, though he was too scared to feel very friendly. He held his hands up, palms forward.

The peasants stopped again, still talking among themselves. The word "*guei*," was repeated even more than before.

"They understand *guei*, at least," said Wayne quietly, slipping one hand back to the belt unit, just in case. "I'm going to try something else."

"Be extremely careful," said Ishihara.

Wayne renewed his phony smile and stepped forward, holding one arm high above his head. He knew they would not understand his speech, but he hoped that they would respond to a friendly tone of voice and gestures of greeting. "Hello, whoever you are. Good evening. We are glad to see you."

The peasants gazed at him. Their eyes were wide with surprise and puzzlement. One of the men in the front, who held a large hoe, shouted to Wayne suspiciously.

"Do what I did," said Wayne. "I think it's working."

"Hello," Ishihara called out. He also raised one arm in greeting. "Good evening."

The peasants watched them without speaking. The man in front lowered his hoe slightly.

"We have to convince them we're good spirits," Wayne said quietly. "Then they'll actually help us."

"If we can prevent them from trying to kill us, I will be satisfied," said Ishihara.

The peasants began talking to each other again.

"It's working," said Wayne. "At least, they aren't as sure as they were a minute ago that we're enemies."

"We have made no aggressive moves," said Ishihara. "That may have helped. However, I recommend again that we jump forward in time and start over."

"Not yet," said Wayne. "This is a populated area, so we might be seen again."

"After dark, that is very unlikely."

"We can use their help," Wayne said eagerly. "We'll need them. We won't be able to speak to anyone else here, either. But we could really use some allies. If we can become friends with them, can you start learning their language?"

"Yes, if we have prolonged interaction with them," said Ishihara. "But I cannot predict how quickly I will make progress."

"I think I remember something from my elementary school days," said Wayne. "Didn't the Chinese used to bow to each other as a greeting?"

"I do not know."

"Well, try it. Do what I do." Wayne caught the eye of the man with the hoe and slowly bowed forward from the waist.

Next to him, Ishihara did the same.

The man carrying the hoe bowed in return. Belatedly, so did several of his companions. All of them fell silent again.

"It's like offering a handshake in our own time," said Wayne. "We finally did something they understood."

An elderly man stepped forward from the group. The man with the hoe joined him, lowering the hoe to the ground. The older man spoke to Wayne, calmly this time.

"Any idea what he said?" Wayne asked.

"No."

"I was afraid you'd say that. But he's asking a question, don't you think?"

"From his tone and facial expression, yes."

"I'm going to guess he's asked who we are or where we came from," said Wayne. He smiled again and pointed to the sky. "I *hope* that's what he asked."

The peasants began chattering excitedly among themselves again. The two men in the front bowed once more. Everyone in the group looked at Wayne and Ishihara in amazement.

"I have to keep this going somehow," said Wayne. "Just follow me." He walked forward, still smiling, and patted his stomach. "Can you help us, friends?" The only tools of communication he could think of were gestures, facial expressions, and tones of voice.

For the first time, some of the peasants smiled in surprise. Certainly, they recognized his gesture of hunger. The two men in the front conferred briefly. Then the older man spoke, waving for Wayne and Ishihara to come with them.

Wayne glanced at Ishihara, relieved. "Well, I got through to them a little. Let's go."

"I would expect the villagers to believe that good spirits who come to visit humans would speak the local human language," said Ishihara. "The villagers may question this."

"Well . . . if they do, we can't understand them. And if we did, we still couldn't explain." With a helpless shrug, Wayne smiled again at their plight. "Since they don't seem to want to hurt us, maybe we can get along."

"I recommend that you keep your hand on your belt unit," said Ishihara, as he joined Wayne in walking forward.

The peasants kept a slight distance from them as they took the road, walking away from the city. They still muttered among themselves and glanced at their new guests with a mixture of awe and fascination. Wayne smiled and nodded at anyone he caught looking at him.

"So how do you feel about this so far?" Wayne asked Ishihara. "Joining them, I mean. They still seem to like us."

"I am most concerned about your safety under the First Law. The danger has only decreased slightly. Our inability to communicate effectively means that a misunderstanding could occur very easily."

"I understand what you mean," said Wayne. "I have every intention of being careful. But I reiterate my ongoing instructions to you: you must help me under the First Law to complete my mission of apprehending at least one component robot. My career and my life in general will be harmed if I can't conduct my own investigation into how MC Governor malfunctioned."

"Acknowledged."

Wayne grinned. "I bet they think we're speaking some sort of fairy language."

"I assume so."

Before long, the peasants left the main road for a narrow dirt path. Ahead, Wayne saw a cluster of tightly bunched, single-story buildings barely outlined by hanging lanterns over the doors. Small children were playing nearby.

The grounds around the village were raked clean, but the surrounding crops had been planted almost right up against the small wooden houses clustered in the center. Only the width of a footpath separated the village from the crops, and the buildings from each other.

The man carrying the hoe called out. The children looked up, and elderly women came out of the houses. All of them stared in wonder at the strangers.

Hunter spent an uneventful night in the front room of the bungalow, motionless but not shut down. At the earliest light of dawn, he heard sounds of activity in the city around the bungalow—people talking, carts and wagons creaking, horses and donkeys clopping, and babies crying. A few moments later, Steve came out of his room.

"I guess nobody sleeps late around here," Steve muttered. "What a racket."

"Marcia and Jane have not stirred yet," said Hunter. "I expect they will soon."

"Yeah. Well, I'll go look for the latrine." Stretching, Steve left the bungalow.

A moment later, Hunter heard Jane and Marcia talking to each other. He waited patiently while all three humans rose, dressed, used the latrine, and washed at the water pump out in the courtyard. Then he joined them. The early morning sunlight angled across the courtyard. The sky was clear and bright, though the air was still cool at this hour.

"Good morning," said Hunter. "You are all ready for breakfast?"

"I'm starved," said Steve, tugging his robe here and there. "I just hope I can get used to wearing this thing."

"I need a shower," said Marcia. "But I don't think they've been invented yet. We can arrange baths later in the day, though."

"I'm ready to get breakfast," said Jane. "And if this is the neighborhood where foreign visitors are common, then we can start looking for MC 5 at the same time."

"Let's go back to the same place where I asked for directions," said Steve. "I kind of promised we'd come back there to eat."

"All right." Hunter turned and led his team out of the courtyard through a gate to one side of the main building. "This is a logical beginning."

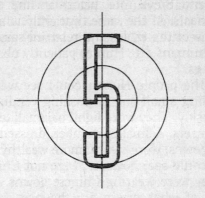

Out on the street, Hunter found shops already open. The aroma of various foods cooking reached him. People filled the street, walking among pony carts and pushcarts.

Steve fell into step next to Hunter. "This is a regular city, isn't it? On an ordinary day. Where would MC 5 go around here to find clothes?"

"As always, I have only approximated the time when he will return to his full size," said Hunter. "I believe yesterday was the earliest; he may not appear for another day or two. I suppose, like the other component robots, he will have to steal clothing when he first arrives, either from someone's trash or maybe from a line of laundry hung up to dry in the sunlight."

A line of people waited at the stall where Steve had asked for information the night before. Long wooden tables and benches had been placed out in front. Hunter could see a big pot of rice gruel simmering over an open fire burning in a brick hearth. Customers bought bowls of the gruel and small plates of pork and chicken strips and fresh vegetables to stir into it.

Hunter and Steve took places in line and bought three breakfasts. At the same time, Marcia and Jane sat down at one of the tables and reserved seats for them. While the humans ate, Hunter patiently observed their surroundings.

Most of the people Hunter could see were Chinese, either tending small shops, pushing vending carts, or walking briskly. They wore light, pajamalike loose jackets and trousers. A smaller number, dressed in embroidered silk gowns, were clearly more wealthy. A very few people he could see, however, were not Chinese at all, though they were wearing Chinese gowns.

"Marcia, of what origin are the two men walking toward us on the far side of the street?" Hunter asked. "In our own time, I would guess they were from the Middle East."

She looked up from her bowl. "That's a good guess. In this era, I'd say they are Central Asian Turks. Starting a couple of centuries ago, several waves of migrating Turks moved westward from Central Asia into the Middle East, which is one reason that many people of this appearance live there in our own time. The Mongol conquest of the entire region has facilitated travel in all directions and, as I said, Kublai Khan has hired many foreigners to work in his government. In fact, these Turks probably arrived by the Old Silk Road, just as the Polo family—"

"That's interesting," Steve said quickly. "But what about them?" He pointed to two men of East Asian ancestry whose gowns were similar to their own, but whose hair was tightly drawn up into a knot on top of their heads. "Nobody else has that hairstyle."

"They're Koreans," said Marcia. "Korea has long been a part of the Mongol empire by this year."

"I think I see some Arabs," said Jane. "They're right across the street."

"Yes, that's right," said Marcia. "The Arabs conquered the Turks some centuries ago and introduced them to Islam. They had some reason to regret it; some of the Turks revolted and overthrew them all the way back to Palestine."

"I'm glad no one's fighting here," said Jane. "I guess Kublai Khan pacified them all, huh?"

"For the time being." Marcia nodded. "But in only a few hundred years—"

"Hunter," Steve said earnestly, interrupting her again. "What are we going to do after breakfast? To find MC 5, I mean? What's our plan of action?"

"This is a good place to begin," said Hunter. "We will start today by becoming familiar with the neighborhood and simply looking for MC 5."

"No reason to stop with that," said Steve. "We can also ask around—maybe offer a small reward to people for giving us a lead on him."

"Marcia, will that be acceptable in this society?" Hunter asked.

"Yes, it will."

"Good," said Steve. "And I guess, based on past experience, we have to keep an eye out for Wayne Nystrom and Ishihara, too. Maybe we should offer a reward for them."

"I agree," said Hunter.

"They haven't stopped you before," said Marcia.

"They have come close," said Hunter. "We must remain alert for them."

The night before, Wayne and Ishihara had shared a modest dinner of white rice and steamed fish in the village. They had slept on pallets in a bedroom in one of the small houses. Though modest, the room was clearly a place of honor; Wayne noticed that the elderly man and his slight, stooped, gray-haired wife vacated it for them and went out to sleep in the main room with seven other people who seemed, by their mutual resemblance, to represent two more generations of the same family. Unable to communicate, Wayne could not protest. In any case, he wanted to maintain the pose that he and Ishihara were good spirits, and he was sure the peasants assumed good spirits would expect hospitality of this sort.

Wayne had fallen asleep quickly, and had slept soundly. When he finally awoke to the sound of roosters crowing outside and people speaking in the main room of the house, he felt well rested but hungry again.

He found Ishihara sitting against the closed door of the room, watching him.

"Morning," Wayne said quietly. "Did you observe anything interesting during the night?"

"No. However, I can announce some minimal progress in learning the local language."

"Really? How?"

"During the night, I have repeatedly reviewed my memory of all our contact with the villagers to this point. At the time we first met them, the First Law required that I focus my attention entirely on the potential danger to you. After I was satisfied that you were safe, I began reviewing the gestures and conversation of the villagers; also, of course, I was able to observe more of their conversation and gestures during dinner last night. When they rose early this morning, I was able to hear some of their speech through the door of our room."

"Wait a minute. I'm no linguist. What's the point of studying their gestures?"

"It was the only way I could begin to pick up vocabulary. For instance, every time someone passed or received a bowl of rice, the word *fan* was used in conversation."

"So you're sure it means *rice*? What if it means, *hungry*, or *more of the same*?"

"You have identified the problem exactly," said Ishihara. "Right now, I am making educated guesses. However, I will begin speaking some of these words and see how our hosts respond. I gave you only one example."

"What else?" Wayne got up and began getting dressed. "More vocabulary?"

"More than that. The basic sentence structure has some similarities to English. The simple declarative sentence goes, subject, verb, object, in that order. When they ask questions, the tone goes up at the end, the same as in English. But the vocabulary is tonal; the lilt you give to each word separates it from what in English would be homophones."

"Okay, okay, I'll take your word for it. But you think you can learn it?"

"Gradually, I will develop some ability to speak with them, yes."

Wayne finished dressing. "Well, I guess it's time for breakfast. Let's go out and try it. And let's see if we can get some local clothes this time."

"Yes, I agree we should do that."

When they opened the door and entered the main room, Wayne saw that it was crowded with people. Everyone who lived in the house turned to look at them, as did as many of their neighbors who could jam inside. Everyone fell silent.

The elderly woman spoke up, pointing to the big pot of rice gruel simmering over the fire.

"*Fan*," said Ishihara, with a casual nod.

One of the younger women picked up a wooden bowl and ladled gruel into it. Another woman spoke quickly to several children, who got up and made room at the hearth. Wayne and Ishihara accepted their bowls and sat down.

Wayne ate in silence, but occasionally he met someone's eyes and smiled slightly. Ishihara, however, attempted to make casual conversation. Wayne knew that Ishihara's ability to learn the language far outstripped his, so he did not try to participate.

He watched with amusement, however, as Ishihara pointed to different people and objects around the room, apparently learning vocabulary. Their hosts were eager teachers, especially the children. Everyone smiled with approval at Ishihara's successful efforts to communicate.

By the time Wayne had finished his second bowl of bland gruel, Ishihara was speaking and gesturing, frequently pointing upward. The villagers nodded with guileless wonder as they looked again at both their guests. Finally the conversation came to a pause.

"What did you say?" Wayne asked quietly.

Their hosts turned to him, fascinated by hearing him speak his strange language again.

"I have made some progress, I believe," said Ishihara. "They are more convinced than ever that we have fallen from the sky as spirits. '*Guei*' appears to mean an evil spirit, maybe an equivalent to a demon or devil. They do seem convinced that we are not *guei*. By the way, all the nouns seem to be collective, without a plural. You may need to pick up a few phrases."

"You seem to be learning the language without much trouble," said Wayne.

"The first stage is the most difficult," said Ishihara. "As I hear more words and more varied sentence structures, my learning curve will rise sharply. Right now I am most effective when discussing physical objects, such as requesting more rice gruel. Concepts such as spirits and demons still make uncertain communication."

The villagers watched them without speaking.

"I want to follow up the idea we had last time—of stopping Hunter and his team first," said Wayne.

"Do you have a specific plan in mind for our current situation?"

"Maybe. Look, if we can interfere with Hunter's team, then we'll have a free hand to find MC 5. When we tried that before, you and I were acting alone. If our hosts, here, will help us in the belief that we're, uh, good spirits, maybe we can really distract Hunter this time."

"We must handle this very carefully," said Ishihara. "I cannot allow any actions that might harm the people of this village or the human members of Hunter's team."

"All we have to do is slow down the bunch of them," said Wayne. "Send them on a wild-goose chase or divide them so that Hunter spends his time trying to gather his team again instead of looking for MC 5."

"By involving the villagers, we increase our chance of altering history in a significant way."

"Well . . . you must admit, we've made numerous small changes already, and so has Hunter's team. Nothing seems to have changed, has it?"

"You and I have not been back to our own time to see if they have had an effect."

"Our presence in Roman Germany had not altered the front between the Germans and Soviets in 1941. Our collective activities in the time of the dinosaurs and in Jamaica in the 1600s, before you joined me, had not made any visible alterations, either."

"Granted, but I insist we must remain very careful. Do you have a plan?"

"Yeah, I think so. Can you tell them that we're looking for Hunter and his team, and that Hunter is an evil spirit we must locate?"

"I believe I can convey that idea," said Ishihara. "But I cannot identify Hunter's human team as evil spirits. Doing so might endanger them too much."

"Then tell them that Hunter, the evil spirit, has duped certain innocent humans into helping him, and they should not be hurt. Is that acceptable?"

"I will tell them that Hunter is a good spirit who is temporarily misguided."

"Yeah, okay."

Ishihara turned to the elderly couple and switched to Chinese. He spoke to them for several minutes, sometimes shaking his head. Finally he turned to Wayne again. "I think I have conveyed my point."

"Are they willing to help?"

"Most of the villagers have to work in the fields. However, some of them are going to the city market with produce to sell. They have no work animal, so they have to pull and push their cart on the road themselves. We can go with them and they will help."

Wayne smiled, nodding approval to their hosts. "Thank you."

Several of them nodded back, also smiling. They seemed to understand his meaning just fine.

*   *   *

Hunter walked through the streets with his team members after they had finished breakfast, with Jane beside him. Steve and Marcia actually led, to maintain the appearance of being the hosts, but Hunter quietly told them when and where to turn. His calculations indicated that MC 5 would probably return to full size somewhere within several particular blocks, rather than on the street, but the margin of error was too large to be certain. These blocks were similar to the ones near the inn—full of small shops and open-air eateries, with peddlers pushing carts up and down the street.

"Jane." Hunter spoke in English. Since they were masquerading as foreigners anyway, being overheard here would not matter. "How do you think MC 5 might have behaved here if he has already returned to full size?"

"Well, these shops have all kinds of stuff, including clothes. He may find something to wear without too much trouble. After that, I don't know. I know that his specialty in Mojave Center was administration of the city."

"Do you think he might move toward the center of government administration here?"

"It would be a logical move for him," said Jane. "But I don't know exactly what that would mean in this society. He'd have to figure that out, too."

"Marcia." Hunter stopped walking. Steve and Marcia turned and joined Jane. "Do I understand that the center of government here is ultimately Kublai Khan himself?"

"Yes, that's correct," said Marcia. "He is surrounded by a huge Chinese bureaucracy, but he is the final authority. In fact—"

"Jane," Hunter interrupted, turning to her. "Jane, would the imperatives of the Laws of Robotics impel MC 5 to seek out Kublai Khan?"

"That's hard to say," Jane said thoughtfully. "Well, let me think out loud for a moment. I was thinking that his own programming as a specialist in city administration would draw him in that direction. But of course, his underlying motive under the First Law would be to lessen the harm to humanity by improving the quality of government."

"What else might he do?" Hunter asked.

"Well, he could get caught up in more mundane First Law activities, I suppose."

"Huh? Like what?" Steve asked.

"Such as helping laborers avoid accidents. Or stopping fights he happens to see. Any sort of individual incident that might attract his attention."

"Sounds to me like we should start spreading the word, like I suggested before," said Steve. "Once we've offered a small reward to anyone who leads us to MC 5, we can just take casual strolls up and down the streets."

"I agree," said Hunter. "You and Marcia will pick the people to approach."

Steve glanced at Marcia. "Let's get started."

"Excellent," said Marcia. "I suggest we offer a graduated system of rewards. To most people on the street, a single copper is worth enough to get their attention. Suppose we offer one copper for someone who reports a sighting of MC 5, two for someone who can lead us to him, and three for someone who brings him to us. If they bring him soon—"

"Hold it, will you?" Steve demanded. "Why do you have to make it so complicated? We can just—"

"Make it up as we go along?" Marcia raised one eyebrow haughtily. "Maybe you're offended that I'm developing your own precious idea."

Startled, Steve fumbled for something to say.

"Please proceed," said Hunter. "Both of you."

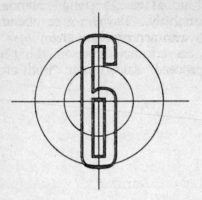

The villagers had already postponed their normal routine in order to visit the good spirits who had graced their village. Wayne urged Ishihara to explain that they wanted to dress as fellow villagers for their walk into Khanbaliq. The villagers seemed amused and honored by this request.

Two men agreed to work in the fields bare to the waist so their guests could wear their shirts and hats. After some consultation, a couple of women reluctantly brought out some old, tattered pants that had been discarded even by the peasants. Ishihara assured them that these clothes were sufficient, and the two of them changed clothes in their room.

Wayne was willing to go barefoot like the peasants, but Ishihara refused to allow this under the First Law. Instead, Ishihara borrowed a knife and cut both pairs of boots he had prepared for Roman Germany down into a sort of makeshift shoes. Then they joined the small group of peasants making the journey into the city. The strongest and healthiest men and women of the village returned to work in the fields for the day.

Lao Li, the village elder in whose house they had stayed, led the others to Khanbaliq. Most of the other peasants who accompanied them were elderly, too, except for Lao Li's twelve-year-old grandson, Xiao Li. Ishihara told Wayne that "Lao," which meant "old," and "Xiao," meaning "little," were common honorific nicknames.

Wayne walked in silence, of course, since no one but Ishihara could understand him. The robot talked with the villagers, often with everyone waving, gesturing, and sometimes laughing as they tried to communicate. Ishihara was learning the language as fast as he could.

As they finally drew near the walls of the city, Ishihara turned to Wayne. "I am making good progress now. One of the villagers has told me that in many of their old fairy tales, good spirits come to earth like this in human form to travel in secret among people."

"That means we fit right in."

"Yes. I am very relieved that we are not, in fact, introducing new ideas to this culture but simply demonstrating existing ones."

"Well, that helps explain why they've been so cooperative, too."

"Still, we must remain very alert to the possibility that we may truly interfere historically with these peasants in some significant way."

"I don't think we have much to worry about," said Wayne. "They're going to market like they do every day, aren't they? We're just tagging along."

By mid-morning, Hunter had led his team up and down every street in the foreign quarter. They passed more Turks and Arabs in colorful, embroidered Chinese gowns, Koreans wearing their topknots and with slightly different embroidery on their gowns, and stocky Mongol soldiers wearing their armor, swords, and daggers. Chinese citizens owned and worked in most of the shops, however, and they were the people most likely to cooperate.

Steve and Marcia spoke briefly to people on every block, describing MC 5. They approached many who worked in shops, but they also spoke to peddlers pushing their carts and to children who were old enough to remember their description of MC 5. Hunter had heard Steve grudgingly agree to Marcia's system of rewards. While they spoke to passersby, Hunter and Jane hung back slightly in their pose as foreign visitors.

They passed merchants of all sorts. The shops and stalls sold fabrics and sturdy, simple furniture on one street and fine porcelains and iron cookware on the next. The third block they visited held stall after stall of different crafts, including a family that was boiling big vats of plant fibers to make paper. On every street, small children ran and played and peddlers pushed carts of small trinkets.

When Hunter realized that the team had seen the entire foreign quarter, he stopped and turned to his companions.

"We have saturated the neighborhood with our offers of rewards," said Hunter. "Since we have been walking for some time, I suggest that we find a place to sit so that you three can rest. We can consider what to do next."

"There's a place back up this block," said Steve. "They're selling tea under the shade of two big trees."

"A tea garden," said Marcia. "That's what the sign over the front entrance said."

Steve glared at her in annoyance. She always seemed to show him up, no matter what he said. For the sake of the team, he decided not to make a scene about it.

"Good idea," said Jane. "I could use a rest."

"I'm hot," said Marcia. "But they don't have cold drinks here, unless you're out in the country and find a mountain stream or something."

"That is fascinating," Hunter said quickly. He found Marcia's spontaneous lectures on local history interesting, but he realized that Steve, in particular, really disliked listening to them.

"Come on." Steve started for the tea shop at a brisk walk and the others followed.

"Shall we just rest up and wait for someone to find MC 5?" Jane asked as she hurried along.

"That is one possibility," said Hunter. "For the first time since our trip to the Late Cretaceous, we have staked out the location where our quarry should return to full size. With the reward we have offered, the number of people around, and the stable nature of life here, we have far more potential help than usual."

"I hear a 'but' coming," said Jane. "I think I know what it is, too. You still can't be sure if MC 5 has already returned to full size."

"That is true," said Hunter. "However, because of his European appearance in a society with very few Europeans, we are not likely to lose track of him completely with our offer of a reward circulating."

Steve turned and waited for them to catch up. "I heard that. We could, you know . . . split up." He grinned.

"That is unwise," said Hunter. "You will remember that in the past—"

"It's a joke, Hunter," said Jane, grinning. "Every time we split up, we regret it. We both know that."

"I see," said Hunter. "Was this joke funny?"

"Skip it," said Steve. "Look, it wasn't totally a joke; I just didn't think you'd go for it. But think about it. Maybe splitting up won't be as bad this time."

"Why not?"

"Well, as you said, life is pretty stable here. Two of us could sit down in a prominent place and wait for someone to bring the good news that MC 5 has been found. The other two could keep up a more active search."

As they reached the counter of the tea garden, Steve turned to order tea for them.

"Has everyone forgotten that we had a plan already?" Marcia asked impatiently. "We were going to look for the Polo family today, remember?"

"I had not forgotten," said Hunter. "I merely raised the question of what to do next. Searching for the Polos is one option."

"All right," said Marcia. "I really didn't think you'd forget."

A young woman led them to a round wooden table under the trees, where they sat down on short, wooden benches.

"I kind of like the idea of meeting Marco Polo myself," said Steve. "Just out of curiosity. But is he really important to what we're doing?"

"We discussed this last night," Marcia said testily. "MC 5 probably knows about him, too, and may also try to contact him. Is that important enough?"

"Yeah, all right," Steve muttered, shrugging.

"When you have rested and finished your tea, I suggest we search for the Polo family," said Hunter.

As Wayne followed the peasants into Khanbaliq, he realized that they knew exactly where to go. They worked their way through the crowded streets to a block of open-air markets filled with fresh produce. An empty stall with wooden shelves and a couple of benches waited for them. Lao Li and his companions quickly moved their produce from their cart to the shelves in the stall.

"Is this place theirs?" Wayne asked Ishihara.

"They rent it. Lao Li complained to one of the others that their rent will be due next week."

"So that means they're in the same place every day." Wayne looked up and down the street. "They must know their neighbors on this block, then."

"I suppose so. Is this important?"

"Maybe." Wayne paused to estimate the length of the city blocks. "We'll want to start spreading the word for people to find Hunter and his team. From what I can make out, the part of the city where MC 5 will return to normal size is fairly close. I think that neighborhood is maybe another couple of blocks east of here."

"That is where Hunter will be."

"Obviously." Wayne looked at Xiao Li, as the boy arranged some stalks of sorghum on a low shelf. "But we don't want Hunter to find out where we are. We'll need some help. Can they spare the kid, here?"

"I will ask." Ishihara switched to Chinese, talking with Lao Li.

Their host spoke with his grandson, whose eyes widened with excitement. Lao Li talked to him in a stern tone of voice. Wayne guessed that he was admonishing the boy to obey these good spirits. Then Ishihara turned to Wayne again.

"He will do whatever we ask. Of course, I cannot allow him to take any significant risks."

"Well, I don't have anything dangerous in mind. I just want him to spot Hunter's team for us without revealing our involvement. Since Hunter can't let him get hurt, either, he should do just fine."

"I agree. What shall I tell him?"

"Ask him what sort of neighborhood lies a few blocks east of here."

Ishihara translated and waited for the answer. "He said it's where the foreign traders and diplomats live. Also many of the foreigners who have taken jobs in the government here."

"I see. Guys like Marco Polo, I guess."

"Yes, that is my impression."

Xiao Li looked back and forth between them, eager to please.

"Well, let's give this a try. Say that we want him to take us over there because we think Hunter may be in that area. Repeat the description of Hunter and also Steve and Jane. Then describe MC 5 and tell the boy that he is even more important than Hunter. And explain that we have to hang back and keep these big hats over our faces so that Hunter won't recognize us until we choose to be seen."

Ishihara translated and Xiao Li waved for them to follow him. Wayne shifted his hat down lower over his face. Ishihara did the same.

The morning had grown hot. After a short walk, Wayne could see that they had reached the foreign quarter; he saw a number of people he guessed were Turks. In any case, they were not Chinese.

Xiao Li looked up at Ishihara and spoke.

"He suggests we sit down at a small corner stall near this spot to have some noodles or tea and wait," said Ishihara. "He will take a quick walk up and down this block for us. If he doesn't see Hunter or MC 5, we'll all walk to the next block and repeat the pattern."

"Tell him that's fine," said Wayne.

When Xiao Li had eagerly hurried off, Wayne shrugged. "Well, since we don't have any money, we can't buy anything. But I'm ready to sit down."

Ishihara pointed to a large tree growing near the street between two small shops. One sold glazed pottery, while the other held cotton and silk clothing. "That spot should be relatively cool. It is not in anyone's way."

"Yeah." Wayne walked over to the tree and sat down, leaning his back against it. His legs and feet hurt, and he would have a long walk back to that village, too, unless they were lucky enough to find MC 5 today. That seemed unlikely, but so far, he was optimistic about their overall chances here. For the first time, he had a team of people helping him to compete with Hunter's team.

Ishihara stood next to him under the tree, looking at the people on the street.

A child's excited shouts got their attention. Wayne looked down the street and saw Xiao Li running toward them with a big grin, waving and yelling as he dodged around other pedestrians. Wayne started to stand, then decided to rest his legs just a moment longer.

The boy stopped in front of them, talking quickly. Ishihara listened, nodding. When Xiao Li finished, he grabbed Ishihara's hand and started pulling him.

"I suggest we go," said Ishihara. "He reports that friends of his have seen Hunter and his team on the next block. In fact, Hunter has widely offered rewards to anyone who can bring them in contact with MC 5."

"Oh, yeah?" Wayne got to his feet. "Well, let's take a look. We still have to stay out of sight, though."

As they started to walk, Ishihara spoke briefly to Xiao Li. The boy nodded and let go of his hand. He led them at a brisk pace, however.

"What did you say?" Wayne asked.

"I told him that running would draw attention to us," said Ishihara. "I reiterated the importance of Hunter's not seeing us until we were ready."

"Good."

Wayne could tell when they were nearing Hunter because Xiao Li slowed down and moved to one side of the street, furtively glancing ahead to the opposite side. Wayne lowered his head slightly so the broad brim of his hat would cover more of his face. Ishihara did the same. The crowd of people and carts on the street gave them plenty of cover.

Finally Xiao Li moved behind the corner of a small noodle shop and pointed diagonally across the street to an area that was shaded with trees. Wayne and Ishihara slipped behind him. Xiao Li spoke eagerly to Ishihara.

"Hunter and his team are drinking tea at a table in the shade," said Ishihara. "I can see Hunter, facing slightly away from us."

"Yeah?" Wayne looked around the corner carefully. He spotted Hunter easily, because of his height and blond hair. Jane sat next to him, blowing on her teacup. Steve sat across from her, next to a woman Wayne did not recognize. She would be the team's historian for this trip, of course.

"See them?" Ishihara asked.

"Yeah." Wayne grinned and gave Xiao Li a quick pat on the shoulder. "Tell him that he will have good luck for doing such a fine job."

Ishihara spoke to the boy, who smiled broadly.

"Now what shall we do?" Ishihara asked. "We do not

have any funds with which to match Hunter's reward."

"That's right," said Wayne. "That reward means real trouble for us. Now Hunter has a lot of people—an uncountable number—working for him now."

"Your plan of distracting him in some way could still work," said Ishihara.

"That's true, I guess," said Wayne slowly.

"I believe so," said Ishihara. "If Hunter is busy and therefore difficult to locate, then his efficiency will still be lowered, even with many people helping in his search. We might increase our chance of finding MC 5 first."

"Let's make sure the story on the street is true," said Wayne. "Tell Xiao Li to approach Hunter and ask about this reward."

Ishihara spoke to Xiao Li, who looked startled. Wayne could see that he was not eager to go near Hunter. The boy turned and studied Hunter for a moment before answering Ishihara.

"He is frightened," said Ishihara. "He is afraid of the bad spirit."

"Remind him that Hunter is not an evil spirit. He's just a good one who is misguided—he should not be doing what he is doing. Give Xiao Li our absolute guarantee that he won't be hurt. Then see if he will talk to Hunter and report back without revealing us."

Xiao Li listened carefully to Ishihara and nodded. Then he took another cautious look at Hunter and slowly walked forward. In the shade across the street, Wayne saw Steve pouring tea again for everyone.

Once Xiao Li reached the tea garden, the traffic on the street blocked Wayne's view of him. After only a moment, however, the boy came hurrying back with a big smile of relief. He dodged the people moving up and down the street and trotted up to Ishihara, reporting breathlessly.

Wayne drew back around the corner of the shop, out of Hunter's sight. "What's he saying?"

"He says it's true," said Ishihara. "Hunter has offered a stepped system of rewards based on how much help he gets. Even the top reward will not make anyone rich, but it is attractive enough to have started many people talking about it on the street. They are searching for both MC 5 and the Polo family."

"Polo family. You mean Marco Polo?"

"Apparently he is here with his father and an uncle, as well," said Ishihara.

"Oh. Well, I don't know much about Marco Polo. Just that he came here in Kublai Khan's time from Italy and went back home to write a book about it."

"I know no more about this than you do," said Ishihara.

"This is the chance we wanted, though," Wayne said suddenly. "Will you tell him to report to Hunter that the Polos have left town? Today, so Hunter thinks he has a chance to catch them. I don't think you should have an objection under the Laws. Hunter will protect his own team."

"Yes, I can tell him to do this," said Ishihara. "However, Hunter will ask which direction they took. Do you wish to develop your ruse further? We have an opportunity to distract him."

"Well, sure. But I don't know exactly what to say. Where is there to send him around here? Someplace convincing that will take him out of way."

"I am not certain. As I told you, I have little knowledge of this society."

"Yeah . . . me, too." Wayne thought a moment. "What

do we know about this time? Marco Polo, Kublai Khan, printing, gunpowder . . ." He looked up suddenly. "Say— what about the Great Wall of China?"

"What about it?"

"Uh, where is it?"

"Perhaps Xiao Li knows." Ishihara turned to the boy and exchanged a few words. "He says it is north of Khanbaliq."

"How far? We want Hunter to go on a long diversion, not just a quick side trip."

Ishihara spoke to Xiao Li again.

"He has heard that the trip takes a couple of days on horseback. Since he has never been there, he does not know for sure how far the Great Wall is."

"That's far enough to get Hunter out of our way for a while. Let's send Hunter there if we can."

"I will tell Xiao Li," said Ishihara.

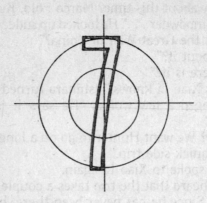

Hunter waited patiently while his companions rested in the shade. Since he regenerated his energy by converting sunlight through the microscopic solar cells on his skin, he had benefited from the walk in the direct sunlight. Certainly this climate, in the summer, was easier on him and his human team members than the Russian winter had been during their last mission.

The little boy who had asked him questions a few minutes earlier walked back, looking at Hunter shyly. He stopped several meters away. Hunter waited for him to speak, but he remained silent.

"May I help you?" Hunter asked.

"I have information for you," said the boy with a polite bow.

Steve looked up from his teacup. "What is it?"

"I have heard that the Polo family went north this morning to the Great Wall."

"Yeah?" Steve grinned. "Hunter, that's great. We know where to find them. And MC 5 probably hasn't had time to reach them yet."

"Are you certain of this?" Hunter asked.

"This is what I have been told," the boy said carefully.

"Who told you?" Steve asked.

He hesitated. "Two men."

"I see," said Hunter. "What is your name?"

"Xiao Li."

"Give him a tip," said Steve.

"A tip is appropriate at this time? What if his information is inaccurate?"

"We'll have to take some risk. Don't give him the whole reward yet. If he's right, we'll pay him the rest."

"Is this acceptable?" Hunter asked Xiao Li.

"Yes, sir."

Hunter reached into his gown and gave Xiao Li a couple of small copper coins.

"Thank you." With another bow, the boy turned away.

"Wait a minute," said Steve. "You might be able to help us with more information."

Xiao Li paused, looking at them all.

"You have more questions for him?" Hunter asked.

"Not yet," said Steve. "But exactly what are we going to do? If we need to change our plans, he might know where we should go to find other people."

"Agreed," said Hunter.

"What is our plan now?" Marcia asked.

"I would like to hear all of your opinions," said Hunter. "I am not certain what to do now."

"This is a stroke of luck," said Jane. She paused to sip her tea. "We could have spent hours trying to find the Polo family and they aren't even here."

"If MC 5 can't find them, then why do we need them?" Marcia asked.

"Good question," said Jane. "But at least we won't waste time looking for them here in the city."

"I think we should go after them," said Steve. "They only left today—probably just a few hours ago. Maybe MC 5 is even with them or following them, too. In order to get some kind of introduction through them to the government, he will have to establish some kind of friendship with them."

"Well, Hunter?" Jane shrugged. "What if MC 5 is here in town, instead?"

"That is a point to consider," said Hunter. "MC 5 is our quarry, not Marco Polo."

"I hate to repeat the obvious," Steve said with a grin. "Especially when I know you don't like it. But this is a stable town and we have no enemies here. Why not split up? Maybe, to reduce your worries, we three should stay here and you can go north to look for the Polos."

"I accepted such logic on earlier missions," said Hunter. "In most cases, I came to regret it. This time, we will stay together."

"Okay." Steve shrugged. "So what's it going to be? Are we staying here to look for MC 5?"

"I remain undecided," said Hunter. "Marcia, how far is the Great Wall from here?"

"About sixty-five kilometers. The road goes north from Khanbaliq through some mountains to a major gate in the wall."

"We would need horses to make the trip efficiently," said Hunter. "On horseback, that is a two-day ride each way, I estimate."

"That's right," said Steve. "At least, depending on how rugged the road is."

Marcia eyed him skeptically. "Oh, you know all about horses, do you?"

"No," Steve said stiffly. "But I have some experience with them. I've owned a couple in the past and used to ride them out in the desert. I can take care of them and I know how far they can travel in a day."

"We rode horseback in Roman Germany," said Jane. "As long as the horses are calm and well trained, we'll be fine."

Hunter was studying Marcia. "Have you ridden horseback before?"

"No," said Marcia uncomfortably.

"Jane is right that safety is largely a matter of matching the horse to the rider," said Hunter. "I will not allow us to go unless we can find one you can ride."

"We wouldn't have to make the whole trip to the Great Wall," said Jane. "If we leave soon enough, we'll catch up to them when they stop for the night."

"That's right," said Steve. "We'll take the rest of today to reach them, talk to them tonight or tomorrow morning, and then return tomorrow."

"This is acceptable," said Hunter. "Spending two days is not extravagant."

"What about Wayne?" Jane asked. "What if MC 5 is still in town?"

"This is a reasonable point," said Hunter. "We could be leaving Wayne and Ishihara two days to find MC 5 here without competition from us."

"The most logical move is to separate, Hunter," said Steve, "no matter how you figure it."

"My interpretation of the First Law at this time does not accept that logic," said Hunter. "My need to protect you overrides the distant possibility that we will find MC 5 by splitting up at this time."

"If the chance of getting MC 5 was clear and immediate, you would allow us to split up?" Jane asked.

"Yes," said Hunter. "The First Law imperative to catch him is stronger than unclear risks to you three."

Steve sighed and finished his tea. "All right. So what are we going to do, then?"

"We must choose between two risks," said Hunter. "If we stay here, we have no current lead to find MC 5. If we follow the lead we have, we may leave Wayne and Ishihara a free hand here to find him first."

"Doing something is probably better than nothing," said Marcia. "I suggest we follow the lead we have to find the Polos."

"Yeah, I agree," Steve said grudgingly, with an annoyed glance at Marcia. "For this reason, Hunter. We've told everybody around here that we're offering a reward. These people, as a group, have a better chance of grabbing MC 5 than Wayne and Ishihara."

"Yes," said Hunter. "We are leaving some help for ourselves behind."

"Good!" Steve got up. "Let's stop wasting time talking about it." He turned to Xiao Li. "Where can we get some horses—four, to be exact?"

"Nowhere in this neighborhood," said Xiao Li. "But I can take you to some stables several blocks from here near the north gate."

"I do not want to take you away from your home neighborhood," said Hunter. "Please give me directions. We will find the location."

Within an hour, Steve rode out of the north gate of Khanbaliq on a small mare, leading the rest of the team. Following Xiao Li's directions, they had found a number of commercial stables in business just inside the north gate. As before, the bargaining fell to Steve. Since no one would lease horses to be ridden out of the city, they'd had to buy them, and of course saddles and bridles, as well.

Hunter had enough money to do so, and the man who sold the horses also told them where to find inns along the way where they could spend the night. Steve had mounted each horse they'd considered buying, to make sure that it was well trained and calm enough for the less experienced riders.

When Hunter's concern for everyone's safety had been satisfied, Steve had found a shop that sold water skins and meat buns they could take with them. Another shop had sold them each long leather coats trimmed with fur for the cold nights in the mountains.

Immediately outside the north gate of the city, the road was deserted in the middle of the day. Steve could see that it wound up into the forested mountains ahead. He turned to look back over his shoulder.

Marcia sat stiffly upright on a seven-year-old gelding, holding the reins gingerly. Hunter rode next to her, giving her instructions. Jane kicked her mount and came up next to Steve at a trot.

"I just thought of a problem I hadn't considered before," said Jane.

"Huh? What's wrong?"

"The man who sold us the horses said we could find inns along the way to spend night, right?"

"Sure. What's the matter with that?"

"Well, the idea was to catch up to the Polos when they stop for the night. But if this road has a lot of inns, we'll have to look for them at every single one."

"I guess we can do that."

"I guess." Jane shrugged. "I just hope we don't find too many inns tonight."

"We'll have lunch in the saddle," said Steve. "The Polos will probably stop by the side of the road to eat, like anyone ordinarily would. If we're lucky, we might even get close enough this evening to see them up ahead. Then we'll see where they stop."

"I guess we can hope."

Steve looked behind them again. Marcia remained tense but said nothing. He considered teasing her about her nervousness, but then decided that he preferred having her quiet. The last thing he wanted was to start her talking again.

The road grew more rugged less than an hour out of Khanbaliq. Tall trees shaded the road as it began to wind up the slope of the foothills. Two riders passed them on the way south, as did one large wagon full of firewood, but traffic was light.

On the road itself, the ground was dry and dusty. Many hooves, wheels, and feet had left their imprints, but to Steve's eye, a few fresh tracks of horses and wheels overlaid the older ones. They had been left by the people who had most recently preceded them. He assumed that some of the tracks had been made by the Polos; he hoped that at least one set were MC 5's. If the team was on the track of MC 5 already, this mission could be really short.

At intervals, Steve offered the buns and a quick drink of water to the others. In order to close the gap between themselves and the people ahead of them, they stayed in the saddle and kept moving.

The air grew cooler as they rode higher into the mountains. Late in the afternoon, Steve paused to put on the long coat he had bought; Marcia and Jane decided to wear theirs, too. The shade of either the trees or the mountains covered them most of the time at this hour.

Finally they rounded a bend and came to an inn. Steve dismounted and asked if any foreigners had stopped for the night; in exchange for a coin, the innkeeper told him that none had. The team rode on.

A much larger inn lay a short distance up the road from the first one. Steve decided that the two inns had been been positioned about a day's ride from both Khanbaliq and the Great Wall. Night was falling quickly now, and the air at this altitude was chilly. He reined in and turned to Hunter.

"See the stable here? This inn has quite a few guests. And it's getting cold pretty fast. I think we should spend the night here, whether the Polos are inside or not. If they found another inn up the road, we can start early tomorrow morning and try to catch them on the road."

"I agree," said Hunter.

"I'll be glad to quit riding for the day," said Jane. "Marcia, how are you?"

Marcia started to dismount, then paused with a grimace. "I think I need help getting down."

Hunter dismounted quickly and reached up to lift her off. He gently set her on her feet. "Are you injured?"

"No. Just sore."

A hostler came out of the stable and Steve arranged for him to take care of the horses. Then they went inside the inn. Entering last, Marcia walked stiffly but without help.

Inside the door, Steve found a large room with a fire roaring in a stone fireplace set into the opposite wall. People were seated around several tables near the fire, eating and drinking. To the left of the door, a slender man with gray hair looked up from the counter where he was carefully writing with a narrow brush.

Steve identified himself again as a scholar seeking an appointment. He requested two rooms for the team as two married couples. The innkeeper took them up to the second floor and showed them the rooms, which were across the hall from each other. They were small but clean and tidy.

Each room had two beds, a large pitcher of water, wash basins, and a chamber pot. Steve glanced at each of his companions; they all nodded. Hunter paid for the rooms.

Then Hunter remembered the group of people sitting near the fire. "Do you have any foreign guests tonight?"

"Foreign guests? No, sir. Not tonight."

"Are all your guests right here?"

"No. A few have finished their dinners already and gone to their rooms."

"I see. Are there other inns nearby?"

"One small inn lies south of here a short distance. The lodgings there are not nearly as comfortable as ours, however, and—"

"We saw it on the way. Are there others?"

"Not within half a day's ride."

"All right. We will be right down in a minute to have dinner for four."

The innkeeper bowed and went back downstairs.

"I'll just leave the bag of clothes up here," said Steve. He tossed it onto one of the beds. "Let's go get some hot food. I'm starved."

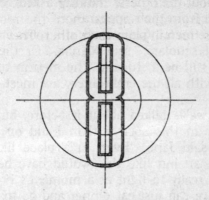

As they descended the stairs, Steve glanced over the other travelers seated at the tables. He had no idea what their clothing signified, except that all of the other patrons appeared fairly well-to-do. Certainly none of them were peasants.

Steve found an empty table in the corner. The other patrons had taken tables closer to the fire. In a moment, the innkeeper hurried out to bring them a pot of tea and teacups, pouring for all of them.

"Are all of these people Chinese?" Jane asked. "Or are some of them Mongols?"

"I don't see any Turks in this group," Steve said with a grin. "At least I can tell that much."

"I would say by their clothing that they are all Chinese," Marcia said quietly. "Here along the border, a lot of genetic mixing has taken place over the years, so you can't really tell by personal appearance."

Steve inclined his head toward a couple of men who wore swords in scabbards at their belts. "Soldiers?"

"Yes," said Marcia. "But they're Chinese soldiers in the army of the Chinese empire, not Mongols."

"What about the others?" Hunter asked. "How much can you tell from their appearance?"

"The three men in plain black silk robes are probably government scholars," said Marcia. "Or the youngest one might still be a student. The men in the colorful silk robes with all the embroidery are most likely rich merchants."

"I know we've talked about it before, but I feel so much safer in this society than I did on our other missions," said Jane. "Even in a place like this. In Port Royal, an inn like this would have been full of buccaneers ready to fight at a moment's notice. Here I feel that we can just eat dinner and go to sleep."

"And those dinosaurs won't show up to trample us, either." Steve laughed.

"It fascinates me," said Marcia. "After so many years studying this era—"

"You just can't believe you're really here," Steve finished for her.

"Well, yes," Marcia said stiffly, glaring at him. "Something wrong with that?"

"Of course not," said Jane. "It's just that all the historians we've worked with said something like that at one time or another. But I know you mean it."

"Take this inn for instance," said Marcia, turning to Jane. "Many Chinese folktales are set at roadside inns just like this one."

"Really?" Jane asked, sipping her tea.

"Some were fairy tales about ghosts, spirits, and monsters; others told of mysterious disappearances." Marcia smiled. "I guess these inns weren't completely safe."

"The people in those stories didn't have positronic robots guarding them under the First Law," said Steve.

*   *   *

Stiff and uncomfortable, Wayne sat in an old, worn saddle on a weary horse, with Ishihara riding behind him on their mount's bare rump. Their peasant friends had somehow bought the horse for them and the saddle and bridle, as well. They were following Hunter's team on the road north out of Khanbaliq. When Hunter's team had first bought their horses, Xiao Li had hidden nearby and watched.

Ishihara had suggested that they let Hunter and his team leave Khanbaliq while they stayed behind to look for MC 5 in the city. However, Wayne had insisted that this kind of logic had ruined his plans before. As soon as Hunter found out that the Polos had not taken the road north, he would come right back. This time, Wayne wanted to sabotage Hunter's team more thoroughly, but he did not know how yet.

The peasants had volunteered to come with them, wanting to earn the goodwill of the spirits they had befriended. Ishihara would not allow it, feeling that a trip of that length would be too disruptive to the village. Wayne wanted their help, but he understood that arguing with Ishihara over this particular interpretation of the First Law was a waste of time.

In the end, Wayne and Ishihara had hidden with Xiao Li to watch Hunter's team ride out of the city. After that, Wayne and Ishihara had waited for Hunter's team to get a head start before following them. They did not want to risk being seen. Ishihara tracked them, instead.

All day on the road, Wayne considered what to do once they caught up to Hunter that night. The best way to distract Hunter had to be to separate him from his human companions up here, far from Khanbaliq.

Then both Hunter and his human team would spend their time and energy trying to reunite. That would leave Wayne and Ishihara a clear opportunity to hurry back to Khanbaliq ahead of them and search for MC 5 without Hunter's interference.

The sunlight in the mountains was fading quickly when they passed a small inn. Ishihara observed that the tracks left by Hunter's team stopped outside but then continued. He and Wayne rode on and reached a much larger inn as night fell. Overhead, however, a high, bright moon offered light of its own.

Wayne reined in. In a small stable off to one side of the main building, he could see a man grooming a horse by lantern light. Flickering light leaked from cracks around shutters on the windows of the inn.

"Did they stop here?" Wayne asked quietly.

"Yes. With my vision altered to maximum light sensitivity, I can just recognize their horses' tracks."

"All right. Now we have to come up with a plan."

"I suggest we move back down the road a short distance to talk. If Hunter turns up his aural sensitivity, he could conceivably overhear us."

Without another word, Wayne turned their mount and slowly rode around a bend.

"This is far enough," said Ishihara. "The wind is slight, but rustles the trees sufficiently to cover our voices from here."

"Good."

"Our own horse has slowed considerably," Ishihara added. "I believe he needs a good night's rest after this trip carrying both of us."

"All right. That's important. It means we can't just jump on and ride him back to the city tonight."

"No. I do not believe he can make it."

"Well . . . we still have to distract Hunter somehow."

"I must remind you that I cannot allow any plan that would harm or allow harm to the human members of Hunter's team."

"I know, I know," Wayne said with exaggerated resignation. "Telling me that is hardly necessary. Besides, I don't want to hurt anybody."

"Another rider is coming up behind us," Ishihara whispered. "I hear light hoofbeats. If we are planning a ruse of some kind, perhaps we do not want to be seen here."

Wayne led their mount into the trees by the side of the road, ducking low under the branches. In the darkness, they did not have to move far to hide themselves. They waited silently. Their horse lowered his head to graze.

Several minutes passed before Wayne heard slow, plodding hoofbeats. Finally the combined silhouette of a small mount and a smaller rider came slowly up the road in the moonlight. Wayne tensed, waiting for the single rider to pass.

"Xiao Li," Ishihara said loudly. "It is the boy Xiao Li."

Xiao Li's shadow jerked in surprise. However, Wayne understood that Ishihara was now worried. They had induced Xiao Li to take an unnecessary risk in following them. Wayne yanked on the reins to pull his horse away from what he was grazing on, and they returned to the road. In the moonlight, Wayne saw that Xiao Li was riding bareback on a donkey, using only a halter and reins.

Ishihara spoke to Xiao Li in Chinese. The boy relaxed, recognizing them. After a moment of conversation, Ishihara switched back to English.

"His relatives pooled their cash from the morning's market sales," said Ishihara. "They bought this donkey for him. All the peasants want to help us. They are absolutely trusting that we will take care of Xiao Li."

"But you told them they couldn't come with us," said Wayne. "What happened? Are the others coming?"

"No. Apparently the villagers decided just to send Xiao Li. They told him to help us out with little errands or anything else he can do for us."

"Well, we'll *have* to take care of him, of course. And maybe we can think of a way for him to help, too."

"I am alarmed by this. I am afraid that we have caused too much change regarding that village already."

"I don't see what we can do at the moment," said Wayne. "We obviously can't send the him away all alone. And we can't just turn around and ride all night back to Khanbaliq tonight, either, on this poor horse of ours. Xiao Li will be safest staying with us."

"Yes, that is true."

"Look, I may have an idea," said Wayne. "But I want to ask you some questions to find out if your interpretation of the First Law will make it objectionable."

"Proceed."

"All right. Will separating Hunter from his human team members harm them?"

"Not necessarily. Of course, that depends on the circumstances."

"Not in and of itself."

"No."

"Will sending Hunter on a diversionary errand be objectionable, in and of itself?" Wayne asked.

"Again, not necessarily."

"Good. I thought so. Then I instruct you to think up

a diversion that will separate Hunter from his team and still be acceptable to you."

"I do not have a precise plan yet, but I can describe the condition our diversion must meet."

"All right. What is it?"

"After we distract Hunter and send him away, I must be in a position to watch over his team, so that I can protect those humans, instead of Hunter."

"Uh, what about me? And Xiao Li?"

"Ideally, you will not be in danger or very far away. But I must know that you are safe, too."

"Okay. Let's see what we can come up with. Suppose Xiao Li goes into the inn and tells another story to Hunter. It worked to get them all up here. Maybe we can split them up somehow that way."

"Hunter has the ability to radio his team for help," said Ishihara. "We will have to take that into consideration also. What should Xiao Li say?"

"As a roboticist, I think the best way to engage Hunter in action will be to repeat what I attempted before—kidnap one of the members of his team. As a robot, do you agree?"

"Yes," said Ishihara. "The First Law requires him to take action, and if I am present to prevent harm to the victim, I can accept this."

"All right. Then, to satisfy you under the First Law, I suggest that you conduct the kidnapping."

"I must agree to the overall circumstances, as well. What will they be?"

"I'm not sure yet, but we'll need Xiao Li to speak to Hunter inside the inn. . . . Tell you what—ask the man in the stable to go inside and see if some other guests will come outside. Maybe we can enlist their help."

* * *

Hunter ate lightly at dinner, just enough to maintain his appearance as a human. Since his energy came from the sun, he did not require food. Even after his team finished dinner, they remained at the table, drinking hot tea.

Marcia had been lecturing them on areas of Mongol and Chinese history that were not immediately pertinent. No one else had spoken for some time. Hunter noticed that the hostler came in and requested that the guests at the other tables go outside with him; Hunter supposed that some minor problem with their horses had developed. Since the hostler had not addressed their table, Hunter gave no importance to the matter.

Steve sat with his arms folded, his cup of hot tea on the table in front of him.

"Most people think the Mongols overwhelmed their enemies by sheer numbers," Marcia was saying. "That's not true at all. In fact, they were often outnumbered in their military campaigns. They won through speed and efficiency."

"Nobody cares," Steve muttered. "And it doesn't make any difference to our mission."

"Well, pardon me." Marcia straightened in her chair. "Perhaps I was mistaken. I thought you might want to learn something for a change."

Steve rolled his eyes and started to get up.

Hunter heard the front door open and saw Steve suddenly freeze in place. When Hunter turned, he recognized the boy from the market coming inside. The boy glanced around and then shyly walked toward them.

"That's the same kid, isn't it?" Steve asked quietly, sitting down again. "I mean, I'm not confusing him with someone else, am I?"

"That's him," said Marcia, folding her arms.

"Yes, it is," said Hunter.

Xiao Li stopped in front of Hunter and bowed politely. He started to speak, but nervously fumbled for words. His face was flushed and he glanced uncomfortably around the table.

"May I help you?" Hunter asked. "I am surprised to see you here, so far from Khanbaliq."

"My family followed you up here from the city," Xiao Li said carefully. "They captured the man you wanted."

"Really? Where are they now?" Jane asked. "Are they outside?"

"They are down the road," said Xiao Li, turning to address her. "At first we told the man to come with us and he did. Then someone must have said something he did not like, because he tried to run away. My family has grabbed him, but he is much stronger than he looks. I rode up here on my donkey to find you."

Hunter noticed that the boy's speech was slow and very mannered, as though he was repeating something he had memorized. That would make sense if the villagers had sent him on ahead with this message. Further, his explanation fit the Laws of Robotics. Initially, if MC 5 had understood he was being ordered to cooperate and come with the villagers, he would have been required to obey. Later, he might have made an interpretation under the First Law from something he saw or heard that gave him the freedom to flee.

"Let's go," said Steve, getting up from the table. "We'll ride down there, grab him, and be done with it."

Xiao Li's eyes widened. "I can't wait for the hostler to prepare your horses. Your friend might escape." He looked at Hunter with large, hopeful eyes. "Please come right away on my donkey with me. Your friends can ride down after their mounts are saddled."

"Good idea," said Hunter, rising also.

"You sure?" Jane asked, as she and Marcia left the table to join him.

"Yeah, what about not splitting up?" Steve grinned as they walked out of the inn with Xiao Li.

"The situation has changed. We are no longer conducting a random search. Now the necessity of apprehending MC 5 while I can is critically important."

"What about our horses?" Jane asked, as they stepped outside into the chilly darkness. "Are we just going to leave them up here?"

Hunter paused. "No. We will give them as gifts to the villagers. They will not return the horses to the city, I realize, but the horses will be back in the same vicinity."

"You better go," said Jane. "We'll ride right down after you as soon as the horses are ready."

"Do not bother," said Hunter. "You will be safer here than riding down this rough mountain road in the moonlight. I will come back with MC 5 and the villagers."

"Whatever." Steve shrugged.

"Our mission appears to be nearly complete," said Hunter. "I suggest that you move up to one of the rooms together and switch on your lapel pins. That way I can communicate with you freely without our being overheard by anyone else."

"That's a good idea," said Steve. "Let's get this finished and go home." He turned and went back into the inn with Marcia and Jane.

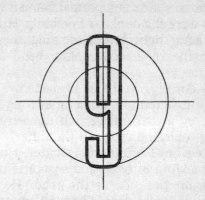

"You're very big for my donkey," said Xiao Li shyly, "but he can carry us both for a short distance."

"We need not burden your donkey further," said Hunter. "I can jog alongside him down the road."

Xiao Li faced his donkey's flank with both hands on the animal's back. He jumped and vaulted forward, landing on the donkey's back with his abdomen. Then he expertly swung one leg around the donkey's rump and sat up, straddling his mount. He kicked it a couple of times and rode off at a trot.

Hunter fell into step alongside Xiao Li and his donkey, concerned that neither the boy nor his donkey could see the road well enough in the moonlight to ride safely at this pace. Since speed was a legitimate concern, Hunter did not suggest slowing down. Instead, he magnified his vision to maximum light receptivity and watched the uneven ground for anything that could trip the donkey.

Hunter and Xiao Li moved down a gently sloping section of road, around a bend, then down a steeper slope. With Hunter's hearing set at a sensitivity in the range of sharp but normal human ability, the only sounds were the donkey's hoofbeats, Hunter's own footsteps, and a light breeze rustling the leaves on the trees as the road took another bend and leveled off.

"I like my donkey," said Xiao Li suddenly. "He's nice. I don't think he's too old. Sometimes I get to ride my uncle's donkey in the village, but not very often. He has to carry tools and crops all the time."

Beneath the boy's unexpected chatter, Hunter heard a sudden crackling of twigs and snapping of branches near him from the side of the road. He turned to look and saw the dark shapes of adult humans leaping out at him. Before he could judge how to avoid them without harming them, they tackled him. Rather than resist and risk hurting them under these unknown conditions, Hunter allowed himself to be knocked to the ground with a thump.

Hunter immediately understood that he had been trapped. Xiao Li's chatter had been intended to cover the sound of the ambushers. Even as the humans who had tackled him grabbed his arms and legs, now shouting among themselves, he surmised that Xiao Li had been given very specific instructions about what to do and say, and that the boy had followed them precisely.

Hunter felt himself lifted off the ground. He discerned seven different voices around him and recognized them all. Each of these humans had been sitting at the tables in the inn near the fire just a short time ago. Hunter did not know what this meant, but he called his team on his internal transmitter.

"Hunter here. Emergency."

Steve said, "What's wrong?"

"I have been attacked by seven men who were in the inn near us during dinner. They are carrying me into the trees near the road. I do not know what they want, but Xiao Li drew me into a trap. Please be very careful."

"Can't you get away," Jane asked, "just by wrestling free of them?"

"Yes, but not without revealing my robotic strength," said Hunter. "I prefer not to do that, since you three remain safe and I am unharmed."

"What should we do?" Jane asked. "Or, rather, what are you going to do?"

"I am undecided," said Hunter. "But I can hear Xiao Li riding away. If you see him, do not trust anything he says."

"Got it," said Steve. "Look, shouldn't we ride down after you? You'd have to protect us and you'd have First Law permission to break free."

"Do not come down here," said Hunter. "I cannot estimate the level of danger to you yet."

"We've survived worse," Jane said. "Remember the fights on the pirate ships? Or the battle between the ancient Germans and the Roman soldiers?"

"Those were different circumstances," said Hunter. "Right now, I have no reason to believe that your endangering yourselves will help find MC 5."

"We still have to get you free," said Steve. "That will definitely help the search, so it should satisfy your objection."

"Please remain where you are," said Hunter. "Entering danger will simply force me into greater First Law dilemmas. It will not help us."

"All right," said Jane. "Steve, he knows more about this than we do. But listen, Hunter. We'll stay here where we can receive your messages freely. Keep us informed."

"Agreed. For now, I must find out what my captors want with me." He broke the connection.

In one of their rooms at the inn, Steve leaned against the door and looked at Marcia and Jane. No one spoke. The only light flickered from a candle flame inside a glass cylinder.

"I can't believe this," Marcia whispered. "What are we going to do now?"

Steve glanced at her, surprised by her anxious tone. A light sheen of sweat covered her face, despite the cool mountain air. She folded her arms across her middle as though her stomach hurt.

"What is it?" Steve asked. "Is dinner bothering you?"

"No."

"You okay?" Jane asked her.

"Of course not! None of us are," Marcia snapped.

"What's wrong?" Steve asked.

"Well—I just—can't you see?" Marcia wailed.

"No," said Steve.

"I think I understand," said Jane. "It's Hunter being out of range to help us, isn't it?"

Marcia nodded tightly. "Of course it is."

"But we're fine," said Steve.

"We aren't used to living without robots around like you are, Steve," said Jane. "Remember? You made a few comments on our first mission about that. I've learned to improvise on these missions myself—and to get along without Hunter right next to me. That's all it is."

"Yeah?" Steve shook his head, looking at Marcia. "She's panicking because Hunter is down the road and doesn't want to reveal his strength?"

Marcia shrugged, glaring at him.

"Well, look," said Steve, "I think we should consider riding down there after Hunter, no matter what he said. We can help him get free."

"I don't think we should," said Jane. "His reasons for waiting were clear. At least, we should call and talk about it with him again."

"We've taken more risk and initiative than that on our own before."

"It's not just us. I'm arguing about this as a roboticist. Hunter doesn't *choose* the First Law; it governs his behavior whether he likes it or not, and he has given us his current concerns and interpretation already."

"If we find him, the First Law will make him free himself to protect us, won't it? Like I said to him?"

"Yes, probably. But there's more to consider. During the last mission, Hunter finally allowed himself to take trips back to our own time in the middle of a mission in order to escape trouble. He'd never done that before. That was a real change in judgment for him."

"What about it?"

"I'm worried that pushing him into a severe First Law dilemma might force him to take us back again. Every time we vanish and reappear, we increase our chances of being seen and we lose some continuity in our plans. In the long run, we might be better off cooperating with Hunter for now."

"Well . . . you're the expert on this stuff," Steve said reluctantly.

"You mean we aren't doing *anything?*" Marcia looked back and forth between them in disbelief. "We're just going to sit and wait?"

"For now," said Jane.

"Let's get some sleep," said Steve, straightening from leaning against the door. "We'll need it tomorrow. You two stay here; I'll go across the hall. Just make sure that your lapel pins are turned on. We don't want to miss Hunter calling again."

"You and Marcia are supposed to be married," said Jane.

"Nobody's going to notice how we divide the rooms," Marcia muttered irritably. "I'll stay with you."

Steve watched her for a moment, tempted to tease her about refusing to play-act her role by sleeping in the other room with him. Then he decided she was already upset enough. With a brief nod to Jane, he left the room, closing the door behind him.

Across the hall, he entered his own room and found enough moonlight shining around the shutter on the window for him to see. Ignoring the unlit candle, he closed the door and undressed. The chilly mountain air also leaked into the room, but he could tolerate the temperature.

In the darkness, under the covers, he found himself tense and wide awake. He could hardly stand Marcia, but the uncertainty about Hunter bothered him, too, in a different way. Marcia felt vulnerable without a robot to protect her. Steve simply felt that he was wasting time, lying here doing nothing while Hunter remained a captive.

Hunter had stopped struggling in order to conserve his energy. He did not know how much strength he would need to free himself. Also, no matter what actions he took, he could not replenish his energy supply until the sun reappeared.

Someone had thrown a cloth bag over his head. It smelled strongly of hay, overwhelming his olfactory sense. Now only his hearing and sense of touch brought him information.

The same seven humans still stood around him, talking excitedly. At this point, only two were actually holding him, one on each arm. Of course, if he pulled free, the others would immediately jump on him again.

The voices around him had been talking for some time, arguing about what to do with him. Most of their chatter had been indecisive and unimportant. However, Hunter noticed that all of them repeatedly referred to him as a "spirit."

Hunter searched his knowledge for the significance of this. At first he thought it might be a colloquial reference to him as a foreigner. He knew that many years later, in the nineteenth century, a Chinese nickname for Europeans and white Americans was "foreign devils."

"We must decide what to do," one man said clearly. He spoke with some authority. "Otherwise, we may argue here in the woods all night."

"Our choices are three," said another man. "One, tie him up in the forest and leave him. Two, remain here and keep watch over him all night. Three, offer him sacrifices of food and wine and give him our respect."

No one laughed. Hunter realized that these were serious choices, not jokes. They really believed he was a spirit of some kind.

"We must chain him while we speak," said someone else. "Away from the road."

The two men holding Hunter's arms pulled him forward. He followed, stepping carefully on the uneven ground to find his footing. His escorts were slower than he was, but they made some effort to guide him, he supposed to avoid tree branches and large rocks.

After a walk of no more than about ten meters, he was stopped and backed up against a tree trunk. He heard the clink of metal and then felt chains pulling him fast against the tree. While his captors muttered to themselves about the exact placement of the chains, he called his team again.

All three of them responded with drowsy voices, at first talking at the same time. No matter which rooms they were in, they all had their lapel pins turned on.

"I have a question for Marcia specifically," said Hunter. "My captors refer to me among themselves as a spirit. However, I cannot reconcile some apparent contradictions. They cannot decide whether to leave me chained to a tree or to make sacrifices to me. The former seems hostile, the latter respectful. Is this choice normal?"

"I can't tell yet," said Marcia. She cleared her throat, yawned, and then spoke with more certainty. "Um, this is related to their local folk religion. It evolves constantly and varies from one geographical location to another, sometimes even between neighboring provinces or villages."

"Oh, wonderful," muttered Steve. "So it's impossible to know what they're thinking at all."

"Let her go on," said Jane.

"It's not totally impossible," said Marcia. "Hunter, what robotic abilities did you exhibit to them? They must have some reason to believe you're not human."

"None." Hunter quickly reviewed all his actions from the time he and the team had first arrived at the inn. "I am certain that I have revealed no abilities to this particular group that are not human."

"Well . . . that won't help us, then. Maybe you resemble a spirit in some folk tale."

"Hold it," said Steve. "You mean, like if someone fit the role of Cinderella?"

"Or King Arthur or Paul Bunyan," said Marcia. "Hunter, from what you've said, they may consider you a good spirit who is misguided or out of control."

"In what respect?"

"Maybe they believe you have been sent here to do something specific that they don't like."

"Yes? What does this mean?"

"Well, this would explain that they want to stop you from fulfilling your instructions from the spirit world—whatever they think those are—but they still want to remain on your good side."

"I understand," said Hunter. "This is consistent with their behavior."

"I have to ask you something, Hunter," said Jane. "Is the Third Law likely to become an imperative soon? That is, are you in danger—or do you expect to be?"

"No," said Hunter. "If the situation changes and the Third Law forces me to escape, I must do it alone without endangering the team."

"Can you reach the belt unit?" Jane asked. "If so, you could return to our time, then come back to this time in another location."

Hunter shifted slightly, testing the chain that held him. "I cannot reach the belt unit without freeing myself. The chain holding me has small links, but I do not know if I can break it or not."

"Your captors haven't taken the belt unit?" Jane asked. "Didn't they wonder what it was?"

"They did not search me," said Hunter.

"That's further evidence that they hold you in some awe," said Marcia.

"What's our current plan?" Steve asked. "What do you want to do?"

"I repeat, do not come to rescue me. I ask that you three get a good night's sleep so that we can be ready to face any unexpected situations tomorrow."

"All right," said Steve. "I haven't slept too well so far, but you're right."

"Okay," said Jane.

"Do you have a plan?" Marcia asked anxiously. "Do you know what we'll do?"

Hunter surmised that she was scared because of his absence. "I am convinced that you are not in danger. Otherwise, I would have to make every effort to free myself. Please get a sound sleep."

"All right," Marcia said reluctantly. "It won't be hard. I'm exhausted after all that riding."

Jane lay back down on her bed in the darkness. She felt her advice in support of Hunter had been justified, but she also worried about him more than she had let on to the others. Marcia was scared because Hunter was not here to protect them, which Jane understood. Steve just wanted to get on with the mission. However, Jane could not stop worrying that Hunter would enter a contradiction between multiple First Law imperatives and be unable to function.

Within a few minutes, Marcia's nervous, uneven breathing became smooth and rhythmic with sleep. Apparently the day on horseback really had worn her out. Jane tried to relax, but she was simply too tense. She lay on her bed, wondering if she had made a mistake in arguing that the team take Hunter's advice.

She had no way to measure the passing of time as she lay awake. However, she remained fitfully awake when a sharp knocking on the main door downstairs startled her. Wondering if Hunter had returned on his own, she listened as the knocking was repeated. Finally, she heard a single pair of footsteps walk across the floor to open the inn door.

More than a few people entered, judging by the number of footsteps. She could not distinguish exactly how many, however. As she heard some quiet voices, too muffled to understand, she realized that these were probably the people who had ambushed Hunter.

All of them remained downstairs. She could hear chairs scraping on the floor, probably as they sat down by the fire again. They probably wanted to warm up after their hike outside.

Since Jane was wide awake anyway, she decided to take a look. She rose and, as quietly as she could, dressed again. If possible, she wanted to overhear anything they might have to say.

Out in the hall, Jane thought about waking up Steve. Then she decided not to bother him. She could wake him later if she learned something important. Otherwise, he might as well get some sleep.

Jane took a deep breath and walked down the stairs. She knew that women had a more restricted role in this society than in her own, but without Marcia to advise her, she had no idea if she was doing something unusual now or not.

Downstairs, she recognized the men sitting near the fire. She counted seven, the same number of captors Hunter had reported. Three wore plain, black robes; two others had embroidered robes; a couple of them wore brown tunics and sword belts. As Hunter had said, they had all eaten dinner there earlier. When a young man in a plain black robe saw her, his eyes widened and he whispered anxiously to his companions.

All of them turned to look at Jane. She forced a slight smile, and nodded to them as she approached. The men by the fire watched her in silence.

Jane could not decide if they were staring because she was a foreign woman alone at this hour or if they simply had not wanted to be disturbed by a stranger.

"Now," said one of the men.

Together, every one of them leaped up and sprang toward her. Before she could call out, one of the men in black robes had clamped a hand over her mouth. Others grabbed her arms and legs, lifting her bodily off the floor.

"Hey—" The innkeeper started, but at the sound of a sword sliding out of its sheath, he fell silent.

Jane twisted around to look at him. One of the men held a sword against the innkeeper's throat. She flailed again, kicking, and realized that she could neither get free nor make enough noise to wake up Steve. With one hand, though, she managed to switch on her lapel pin. Hunter would hear whatever noises her communicator happened to transmit.

Jane's captors marched her out of the inn, into the cold night air. They held her faceup, and over the silhouettes of their heads and shoulders she could see the moon and the tops of trees against the sky. She could tell that she was being carried down the slope, in the same direction Hunter had gone with Xiao Li.

Steve dozed fitfully. The long ride on horseback had tired him, but leaving Hunter chained to a tree for the night bothered him. He understood Hunter's desire to be left alone for now, but that didn't help him sleep any better. When footsteps pounded up the stairs, he woke quickly.

Suddenly Steve noticed static hissing from his lapel pin. Before he could listen more closely, whoever had just run up the stairs thumped on his door. Steve picked up his robes to hold in front of him and found his way to the door in the darkness.

"Who is it?"

"The innkeeper, sir."

Steve opened the door a crack. "What's wrong?"

"One of your companions, sir. The foreign woman with the brown hair." The man held a burning candle on a small tray. The light of the flame flickered over his face, which was lined with fear.

"Jane? What about her?" Steve's worry was followed by a surge of adrenaline. Something had really gone wrong.

"The other guests carried her out of here—by force! With a hand over her mouth and a sword at my throat, I could do nothing, I assure you—"

"I believe you," said Steve, fumbling his robes on as quickly as he could. He stepped past the innkeeper to rap on Marcia's door. Then he remembered that they were supposed to be married; the innkeeper would expect to see Marcia in his room. "Excuse me, will you?" He found a coin in his robes and gave it to the man.

"Thank you! I promise you, sir, I had no choice— this is a fine inn. Nothing like this usually—"

"Please *excuse* me, all right?" Steve demanded, taking the candle from him.

The innkeeper bowed quickly and hurried away.

"Marcia."

"Hmm?" She sounded sleepy.

"Is Jane in there?" He tried the door and found it unlocked. Slowly, he opened it only a little. "You decent?"

"Come in. I'm under the covers. Uh—no, she isn't here."

By the light of the small candle, Steve saw Marcia move up on one elbow and draw hair away from her face. The room was essentially the same as his. Jane's bed had been disturbed, but was empty. He did not see her clothes anywhere.

"What's going on?"

"She's been kidnapped, too. Get dressed and bring your coat. I'll wait out in the hall."

"*What?*"

"Hurry up." Steve backed into the hall again and closed the door. He got his own coat out of his room and picked up the cloth bag, as well. The need to improvise meant that they might not be coming back. He would call Hunter as soon as he had spoken to the innkeeper again.

Marcia joined him, fully dressed but much more groggy than he was. She had obviously been sleeping soundly. He hoped this meant she wouldn't lecture him all night.

"Did Jane leave anything in the room?"

"No."

"She must have gotten dressed for some reason. Come on." Steve led her downstairs, where the innkeeper was anxiously warming his hands by the fire.

"Where are we going?" Marcia asked, her voice still rough with sleep.

"I'll tell you outside." Steve turned to the innkeeper. "Can you tell me anything else about what happened?"

"Not very much, sir. The other guests came back in rather late and sat down by the fire to warm themselves. Then your friend came downstairs—"

"On her own?"

"Yes, sir. She just walked down here, and they got all excited and grabbed her. They ran outside with her. As

I was saying, I had a sword to my throat, or else—"

"Yes, I understand that." Steve thought for a moment. Freeing Hunter was now a necessity. If Hunter couldn't break the chain holding him with his own strength, then Steve would have to help. He pointed to the poker leaning against the side of the fireplace. "I want to borrow that."

"Eh? What's that, sir?"

Steve walked over and picked up the poker. "I'll need this. Do you mind?"

"Begging your pardon, sir, but of course I will be needing it, too."

"Yeah, all right." Steve pulled out a couple more coins and tossed them to the innkeeper. "I'll bring it back when I'm finished with it."

"Thank you." The innkeeper bowed again.

"Let's go," Steve said to Marcia. They hurried outside into the cold mountain air and walked a short distance from the front of the inn.

"Are we going to get the horses?" Marcia asked.

"Uh, no. Too noisy. I'm not sure exactly what happened to Jane, but we have to stay out of everyone's sight if we can, until we find out. We'll have to find Hunter on foot." Steve turned on his lapel pin. "Hunter, Steve here."

"Yes, Steve."

"Jane's been kidnapped. From what the innkeeper said, I guess it's the same bunch of people who jumped you."

"I suspected something of the sort had happened to one of you—"

"What? Why didn't you call and wake us up?" Steve was startled. "You've just been sitting there, even under the First Law?"

"I have been puzzling over how to respond. For only the last few minutes, I have been receiving static and the sounds of footsteps and breathing from someone's lapel pin, but nothing more clear than that. I did not call because I fear, even now, that her captors are listening to our voices coming out of the air and will be even more fearful than before. Once you called me, however, the damage was done. I must have your help to free myself."

"Where are you?" Steve asked. "Are you alone, for that matter?"

"I have been left alone, chained to a tree," said Hunter. "I have no way to convey my exact location."

"You can't free yourself?"

"No. I have ascertained that I cannot break the chain on my own. Until I heard the unexplained static, I had intended to wait until after dawn to try again. At that time, my energy would be replenished, and I could awaken you three without disturbing your rest."

"We'll come get you," said Steve. "I have a fireplace poker; maybe we can use it to pry open a link of your chain. How can I find you?"

"Follow the road back down the slope. When I hear you nearby, I will call to you."

"Okay. But I'll leave my lapel pin on." He turned to Marcia. "Come on."

"It's freezing out here," Marcia muttered.

"Well, it'll help keep us both wide awake."

Ishihara and Wayne had hidden themselves near the road about halfway between the place where Hunter was chained and the inn. Xiao Li stood with them, holding the reins of his donkey and also the horse Wayne and Ishihara had ridden from Khanbaliq. They had to stay far enough from Hunter so that he could not hear their voices.

Earlier, after Xiao Li had asked the other guests in the inn to come out and speak to them, Wayne and Ishihara had given them the same story that Xiao Li and his fellow villagers had accepted, that Hunter was a misguided spirit. Some of the guests had been skeptical about this, but the more superstitious men among them had convinced the others to consider it. Finally, Wayne had assured them all that Hunter was absolutely prevented by supernatural law from harming humans, but that he had to be restrained.

"We have to figure out what to do next," said Wayne. "We have Hunter. He'll probably radio his team to come get him, but maybe we can interfere with that, too—"

"I have an emergency," Ishihara said abruptly. "I have been monitoring Hunter's radio band to intercept his communication with his team members."

"Yeah? What of it?"

"Steve has just reported to Hunter that Jane has been kidnapped from the inn by the same guests we convinced to take Hunter. They obviously saw them together and acted on their own."

"But that's good," said Wayne enthusiastically. "It'll keep the whole team busy. Why didn't they grab the other two, while they were at it?"

"It was apparently a spontaneous move. However, I now feel that I am responsible for potential harm to Jane. Under the First Law, I must rescue her."

"Well . . . wait a minute," said Wayne. "Let's think this through."

"I cannot wait." Ishihara turned and began working his way out of the trees to the road. "A further consideration is that her captors will have overheard the voices of Steve and Hunter through her lapel pin, which seems to have remained turned on. This could endanger her even more."

"We can still talk about it," said Wayne. "This isn't necessarily bad. At least, let's consider the whole situation before we act."

"The First Law will not allow me to wait," said Ishihara, over his shoulder.

"Well . . ." Wayne plunged after him, crashing through the underbrush. "Then wait for me."

"Please hurry," said Ishihara. "The only transmission now is background static and the sound of humans breathing and walking. However, this tells me that they are coming down the road toward us from the inn."

Wayne pushed his way through tree branches after Ishihara, panicked by the danger of losing his only ally. Certainly, Ishihara could rescue Jane, and Wayne did not object to that. However, as a roboticist, she might very well argue First Law interpretations with Ishihara that would convince him to stop cooperating with Wayne.

Behind him, he could hear the sound of Xiao Li following, bringing the horse and the donkey.

"Shut off your hearing," said Wayne urgently to Ishihara, as he finally managed to come up next to him on the road.

"I dare not. My First Law imperative to rescue Jane requires all my efforts." Ishihara strode quickly up the road in the moonlight.

"I don't want Jane to trick you. She may argue that you should help Hunter instead of me."

"If her arguments are valid, I will respond. If they are not, of course I will not be influenced."

"Well . . . all right. But remember, Jane's arguments about cooperating with me do not involve Jane's personal welfare in this particular situation."

"I accept your instruction."

Wayne said nothing else as he hurried up the slope. He knew that while every robot had to obey the First Law, each one had some leeway to make independent interpretations. All Wayne could do now was try to influence him.

Since Jane's captors did not speak as they carried her through the cold night air, she did not learn anything about what they had in mind. They were still taking her in the same direction Hunter had gone, so she was not really too scared. Before they had gone very far, however, the men carrying her suddenly stopped. Jane heard the voices of Hunter and Steve coming over her lapel pin, muffled slightly under a fold in her rumpled robe. Suddenly very frightened, she forced herself to cough and clear her throat, in the hope of covering the sound.

"What's that?" One of the men asked fearfully.

"What's what?" Another asked.

"Voices."

"I hear them, too," said a man near Jane's left shoulder. "Voices from the air. No—from her!" He released his grip suddenly and she began to fall.

"Let her down! Let her down!"

Jane felt herself lowered; at least they had the decency to set her on her feet. When she found her footing, she looked up and saw all the men slowly backing away from her in the moonlight. Then another pointed past her, down the road.

"Look! Someone's coming! Who are they?" He spoke in a hushed, worried voice.

"Maybe it's the big spirit," yelled a third, "coming back for her!"

With a roar of frightened shouts, every man who had carried Jane to this spot suddenly turned and ran back up the road. Puzzled, she glanced down the road to see if Hunter had somehow gotten free. Instead, two other figures were running up the slope toward her.

At first she had no idea who they were. Then, even in the moonlight and shadows, she recognized Wayne and Ishihara. Xiao Li, mounted on his donkey and holding the reins of a horse, waited without moving behind them.

She had to choose between dealing with them, following the others back up the slope, or running into the forest. She did not really want to face Wayne and Ishihara without Hunter. However, she knew that their company would certainly be safer than that of her recent captors.

After all, no matter what argument Wayne had used to bring Ishihara under his control, the First Law would still require the robot to protect her from actual harm. If she could convince Ishihara to drop Wayne, then she would have accomplished something important, too. So she waited for them to come running up to her, checking to make sure that her lapel pin was still on.

She did not want to speak directly to Hunter now, while Ishihara could hear her. If Hunter could hear them through the lapel pin, he might find a way to help. In that case, he would want the element of surprise.

"*Now* shut off your hearing," Wayne ordered Ishihara, as they drew near. "And don't read her lips, either."

"I already told you I cannot do that," said Ishihara. He stopped in front of Jane.

"That was when she was a captive," said Wayne. "Now she's okay."

"Jane, are you harmed?" Ishihara asked.

"No," Jane said sternly. "I'm not. But I don't owe any thanks to you for that."

"I had nothing to do with your being kidnapped," said Ishihara, his voice conveying just a hint of urgency. "Neither did Dr. Nystrom. I have not violated the First Law."

"No?" Jane put her hands on her hips, assuming the tone of schoolteacher challenging a naughty child. "What are you doing cooperating with him at all? Hunter told you that his missions are driven by a First Law imperative."

"Don't listen to her," Wayne insisted. "I told you that Hunter's argument is full of holes."

"Ishihara, take custody of Wayne on behalf of Hunter's First Law duties," said Jane. Then, still hoping that Hunter was listening, she tried to help give their location. "Since we're only a short distance down the slope from the inn, the rest of my team is not far."

"I cannot. The imperatives under the First Law are not clear to me on either side. I wish to convince you, however, that your kidnapping was never part of our plan. The guests at the inn acted on their own."

"Well, I sort of guessed that," said Jane. "But you must have told them something that set it up."

"That is true," said Ishihara. "I am relieved that you are well."

Xiao Li, who was still leading a horse, joined them on his donkey, but did not speak.

"Look," said Wayne. "We have to talk, but not here. Ishihara, take her lapel pin and shut it off."

"No!" Jane ordered, stepping back. "Stop. This will harm me."

"I will not allow harm to come to you," said Ishihara. He reached out and took her lapel pin.

Jane did not bother trying to wrestle with the robot. "What do you want with me, Wayne?"

"Ishihara, we have to get away from here before her team comes after her. Bring her."

"Hey! You can't do that." Jane backpedaled again, but she knew she could not outrun Ishihara any more than she could wrestle with him. Her only chance was to argue. "Ishihara, this constitutes harm. I need sleep and I need to rejoin my team. You must see that."

"I cannot harm you." Ishihara gently took hold of her arm. "Further talk in private will not harm you."

"Say," said Wayne suddenly, "Steve is marching around here somewhere looking for Hunter. He probably has their historian with him. Can you grab them, too?"

"No," said Ishihara. "I could not keep control of three humans without risking harm to them."

"Well, all right, then," said Wayne, glancing up and down the road anxiously. "Let's get off the road and into the brush. Fast."

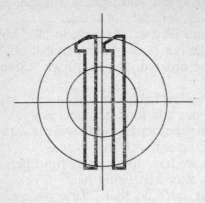

Steve led Marcia down the side of the road, keeping to the shadows as much as possible. Since they had kept their lapel pins on, he and Marcia had overheard the reaction of Jane's captors to his last conversation with Hunter. A moment later, they'd also listened to Jane's exchange with Wayne and Ishihara, up to the moment her lapel pin had been suddenly switched off.

"Jane's in serious trouble now, isn't she?" Marcia asked quietly.

"Well, at least she's safe with a robot," said Steve. "Hey, look up ahead."

Steve saw the growing shadow of a large group of people down the road. They were running up the slope toward Steve and Marcia. Quickly, he grabbed Marcia's arm and pulled her into the trees, then crouched with her in the underbrush.

"Quiet," he whispered.

She nodded.

The group of frightened men, breathing hard from the exertion of running up the mountain road, pounded past without seeing them. In another moment, they had rounded the next bend back toward the inn. Steve stood up, pulling Marcia with him, and returned to the road.

"Well, *I* think Jane's in trouble," Marcia whispered. "We have to rescue her, don't we?"

"We have to get Hunter first."

"Do we have time? What are these other two going to do with her?"

"Ishihara can't violate the First Law any more than Hunter can, so Jane won't be harmed. But he must be following Wayne's instructions, which means that he won't let us just take her away, either."

"How can you be sure?"

"Because Jane wants me to get Hunter, too."

"Oh, come on. She didn't say that."

"She couldn't say it plainly without giving away the message to Wayne and Ishihara."

"So what makes you think you heard it?"

"She knew her lapel pin was on, until one of them took it. If she had wanted us to come running, she could have yelled for us. Since she didn't, she was telling me she was okay for now."

"But how do you *know* that?"

Steve sighed. "Because I've worked with her long enough now to know how she thinks."

Marcia finally fell silent again.

As they walked, Steve tried to figure out what Wayne would want to do now. He had no way of knowing exactly where Steve and Marcia were, though of course Ishihara would have picked up his recent conversation with Hunter. So they knew Steve and Marcia were out here looking around.

Wayne might be hustling Jane farther down the mountain road, going south, or taking her out into the forest itself. Then again, he could have ordered Ishihara to grab Steve and Marcia, too, though Steve doubted that a single robot could hold all three humans captive at once. Most likely, Wayne and Ishihara were running away with Jane while they had the chance.

In any case, as Steve and Marcia hiked down the road, they saw no sign of them.

"Steve," Hunter called from the trees. "This way. Follow my voice."

Steve turned carefully toward the sound, picking out the direction. Hunter called out repeatedly so that they could find him. Steve glanced back to see that Marcia followed him through the branches and underbrush, then pushed forward.

After a few minutes of hiking on rough, uneven ground, they reached Hunter. Hardly enough moonlight to see anything reached them here. Steve looked up high at the silhouette of Hunter's head.

"Aren't you even taller than usual?"

"Yes. I made myself as tall and thin as I can, to loosen the chains. However, I was still not able to get free. I can move my arms somewhat, though. Do you have any more information now about Jane?"

"Not really," said Steve. "Except that she didn't scream for immediate help."

"Ishihara will protect her, of course. You have the poker you told me about?"

"Yeah. But I don't suppose I'm strong enough to do much with it."

"Give it to me. I have enough freedom of my arms now to use it."

Steve felt for Hunter's hand and placed the poker in it. "You want me to do anything?"

"Yes. I have felt the individual links of the chain I can reach already. In my other hand, I am holding the weakest one. These are not, after all, mass produced. As I hold the handle of the poker, please fit the point of it into the middle of this other link."

"Okay. Let's see. . . . Got it."

"Please stand back. I will use the curve of the tree trunk as a fulcrum and attempt to pry the link open."

Steve backed away, moving Marcia with him. If the end of the poker slipped out of the link by accident, the point could swing around and club them both. Steve could barely see Hunter's movements, but after a long moment, he heard the chain fall, clinking, to the ground.

"Finished," said Hunter. "I will return to my previous appearance."

"Now what are we going to do?" Marcia asked.

"I shall attempt to locate Jane," said Hunter. "I believe that Wayne and Ishihara arranged to have me trapped in order to break up our team and waste our time and energy. However, I am certain that they expected me to remain isolated much longer. They will not expect you to have released me so soon."

"The trouble is, now that they have Jane, we're still split up," said Steve.

"How are you going to find her?" Marcia asked. "Her lapel pin is turned off."

"I am turning up my hearing to maximum," said Hunter. "As we walk on the road, I believe I should be able to hear Xiao Li's donkey. If they are moving through the underbrush, the donkey will make more noise than the humans. If the boy rides him on the road, I may hear his hoofbeats."

"Let's get back out on the road," said Steve.

* * *

Jane said nothing as Ishihara led her slowly through the dark forest by a gentle but firm grip on her arm while Wayne walked beside them. She heard Xiao Li following them, walking the horse and donkey now that they were moving among the trees once more. Ishihara walked slowly, changing direction to avoid trees, boulders, and dense clumps of underbrush. When they finally stopped, she had no way of judging how far from the road they had gone, but she doubted it was very far. She waited to see what Wayne and Ishihara would do next.

"Have you heard any communication between Hunter and Steve?" Wayne asked Ishihara.

"No. I am surprised. I would expect Hunter to send a constant signal, so that he could be found. Or else I would expect ongoing conversation between them. I do not understand what they are doing."

Jane saw Wayne turn to her in the faint moonlight.

"We haven't really had a chance to talk, have we?" Wayne asked, in a casual tone.

"No. That's true." She could barely see his silhouette in the moonlight that filtered through the leaves overhead. "What do we have to say to each other? Anything?"

"May I speak to you as one roboticist to another?"

"What choice do I have?" Jane demanded. She could afford to take a hostile tone with Ishihara here to protect her.

"I just want to explain something to you."

"Well, I'm waiting."

"I only want to participate in the review and investigation of the Governor Robots." He waited for her response.

From the R. Hunter files

The now-famous prototype of the highly successful "Hunter" class robot first demonstrated his remarkable abilities in the Mojave Center Governor case. The following images are drawn from the Robot City archives of Derec Avery, the eminent robotics historian.

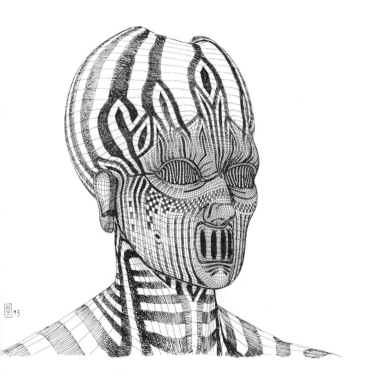

The Mojave Center. An aerial view of the Center, including the Governor's Building (foreground left), complete with stadium on top; the Bohung Institute (background center), which is surrounded by a park in front and a gorge with redwood forest and waterfall in the rear; and the Residential Building (right), with its water park inset on the wall: lake, river, waterslides and kayaks, trees, and grass, plus a sculpture garden on the side.

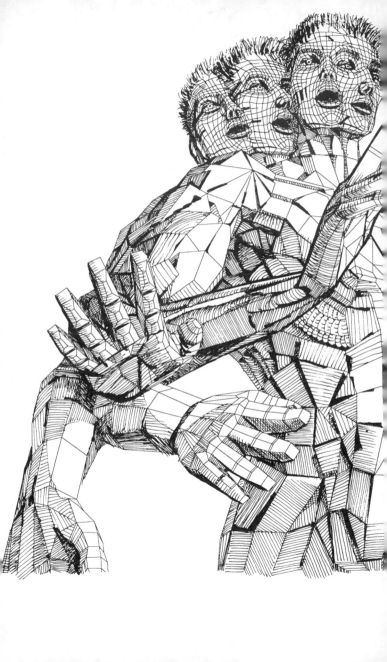

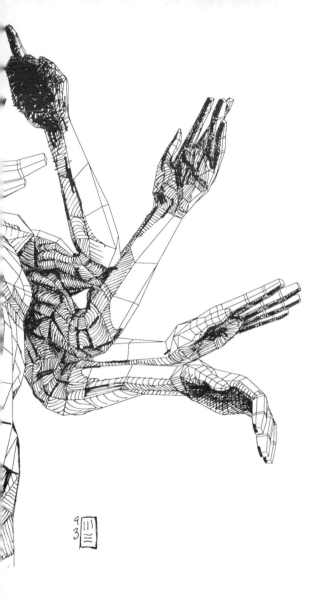

MC robots merged. Four of MC Governor's six independent component robots are shown here. After capturing them in the remote past, R. Hunter merged and deactivated the robots temporarily.

Governor's Building. The bank of elevators on the "Transition Plane" level. The "90°" label indicates the direction relative to North one is facing (in this case East: ninety degrees from North).

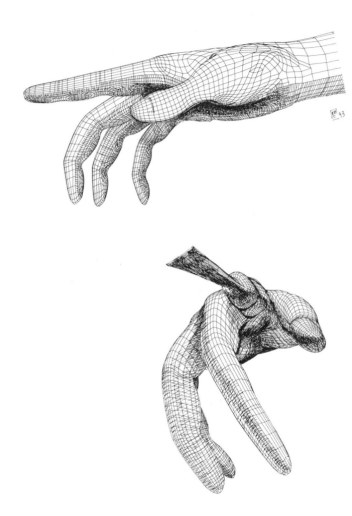

R. Hunter's hand. Here we see the versatility of R. Hunter's manual
extremity. Clockwise from top left: as a normal human hand;
extended and upturned to be used as a crowbar or pry; as an awl,
which can be used as a pick or as a weapon; and as a flathead screw-
driver.

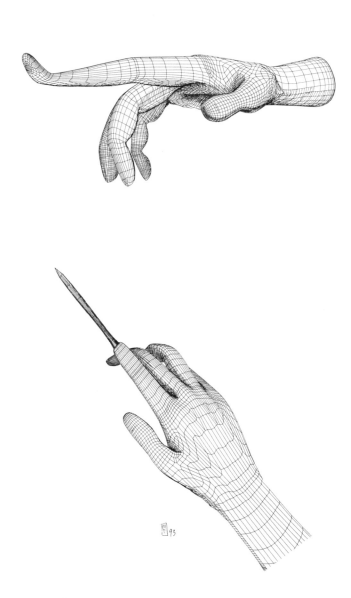

The Mojave Center. A ground's eye view of the Center's "downtown," including (l.-r.) the Residential Building, the Central Computer Memory Building, the Communications Station, the Genetic Engineering Center (a.k.a. "The Helix Building"), the Office Building (with park atop), and the Governor's Building.

The Gate to the Forbidden City. R. Hunter, Steve, and Marcia are led by Marco Polo into the grounds of Kublai Khan's palace.

The Cliffs. A mall in the Mojave Center, located in the lower portion of the Governor's Building, complete with escalators and moving sidewalks. It is from here that the clothes and supplies needed by the time travellers are procured.

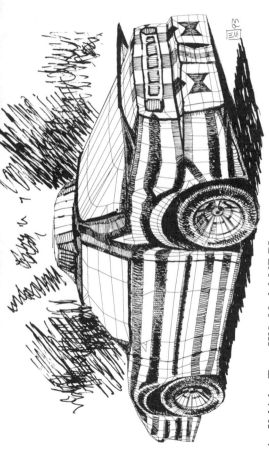

Mojave Center Security Vehicle, Type W5, Model ME-BJ.
Equipped with a low-level positronic brain, this vehicle can adapt its shape and wheels to fit any terrain and transport up to eight people or robots. It has a maximum speed of 325 kph. The roof protrusion contains full-spectrum scanning equipment. The body is capable of withstanding heavy fire from any known hand-held weapon or ground assault vehicle.

"Go on." She tried not to react outwardly.

"I can't allow total strangers to take over my work and pass judgment on it without me. These robots are my creation. You understand that."

"Yes," she said stiffly.

"The problem is not science and engineering, but politics. I have no bargaining power unless I hold at least one of the component robots in my possession."

Jane said nothing.

"What's objectionable about this?" Wayne demanded. "Don't you think I have a point?"

"It sounds reasonable enough on the surface. How do I know that's the whole story?"

"You don't trust me?" He sounded genuinely hurt.

"You've *kidnapped me*. What do you expect?"

"Wait a minute. Have you forgotten that trip we all made to Russia in 1941?"

"Of course not."

"I saved both that other woman on your team and Steve from being shot by a Nazi guard—when I had a clear chance to get MC 4 instead." His tone turned bitter. "Or didn't any of you *notice?*"

"Of course we did." Jane felt a little embarrassed. "Everyone noticed—and I thank you for all of us. And I know I won't be harmed with Ishihara here. But why don't you consider just coming back and discussing the situation professionally?"

"No!"

"I think the Oversight Committee will be responsible. They should be allowed to do their job."

"This is logical," said Ishihara.

"Hold it right there," Wayne said angrily. "I can't afford to gamble my entire career on the committee's integrity. I told you, I need independent bargaining power. And a chance to examine MC 5 myself, without interference."

"Listen to him, Ishihara," said Jane. "You can see he isn't being reasonable. You can't possibly have a valid First Law reason to keep me here."

"Remember what I told you," Wayne ordered sternly. "My First Law argument to you concerns the unnecessary harm Hunter's team is doing to me. That's the argument you accepted when you first agreed to help me on these missions."

"That is true," said Ishihara.

"What's true?" Jane demanded.

"I cannot shift my Second Law loyalty to you," said Ishihara. "I have accepted the possibility that Wayne is being harmed by the actions of Hunter and his team. He requires my aid as a result of this."

"All right, look," said Wayne. "Since I can't convince her I'm right, she'll have to come with us for a while. We have to get away from here, so Hunter won't be right behind us every minute. Let's go find MC 5."

"You mean return to Khanbaliq?" Ishihara asked. "Our horse is exhausted. The animal cannot make the return trip tonight, nor can the donkey. You and Xiao Li and Jane will need rest as well."

"We don't have to go all the way back tonight," said Wayne. "But I want to get started. Then we'll find a place to sleep for the night."

"It's too cold out here to get much sleep," Jane said sourly. "We don't have any protection from the elements. That's not very good protection from harm, Ishihara."

"We'll manage," Wayne said quickly. "Ishihara, you take charge of our route. Include evasive action to avoid Hunter. Jane and I will not be harmed by a night in this weather."

"My options are limited," said Ishihara. "Fleeing through the forested mountains in the dark is highly dangerous to you and Jane."

"Do what you can," Wayne said sternly.

Steve brought up the rear as Hunter led the way through the trees back to the road. Marcia walked with her arms wrapped around herself, shivering from the cold. Out on the road, Hunter waited for them.

"I want to change frequencies now that we know Ishihara is listening," said Hunter. "He has always listened in when we're in the same time period together." He altered the settings on their lapel pins. "I hope we will not separate again, but we must be prepared."

"He'll just scan the frequencies again, won't he?" Steve asked.

"I assume so. However, we will not use the lapel pins often, so he may simply stop scanning because it wastes his energy. If he happens to scan the radio band when we are communicating through these, he'll locate the new frequency, but perhaps not immediately. Any delay we can create in being overheard will help us."

"Okay." Steve shrugged. "You know more about what a robot does than I do."

Suddenly Hunter straightened, turning to look down the road, to the south.

"What—" Marcia started.

Steve put a hand on her shoulder to quiet her. He heard nothing and could not tell if Hunter heard something or was receiving a radio transmission. Either way, Hunter certainly did not need any distractions. Marcia shoved his hand away but said nothing else.

"I hear two sets of hoofbeats cantering down the road, back toward Khanbaliq," said Hunter.

"Two sets," Steve repeated. "Shouldn't there be at least three? Wayne and Ishihara must have ridden up here on horseback, plus Xiao Li's donkey."

"And Jane is riding double with someone," Marcia added. "I see."

"I hear two animals," said Hunter. "One much smaller than the other, matching the gait of Xiao Li's donkey, but the hoofbeats are heavier than before. That one is certain; two people are riding the donkey."

"What about the other one?" Steve asked.

"By the gait and the weight, it is a horse," said Hunter. "I cannot be sure if it is carrying two riders without having heard its hoofbeats earlier. It could simply be an usually large, heavy horse."

"You think two people are riding the horse, too?" Steve shrugged. "I guess it's possible."

"Wayne and Ishihara could have found a mount as easily as we did," said Hunter. "Perhaps financial limitations confined them to one horse."

"Those mounts are worn out from a long day's ride already," said Steve. "If they're both carrying two riders, they won't go far tonight, especially at a canter. They may not go far at all."

"I have considered that," said Hunter. "I suggest that I begin jogging after them from here to maintain aural contact. You two can return to the inn for our horses and bring them. I know they are tired, too, but they will be able to carry us at least as far as the two mounts we are pursuing."

"That makes sense to me," said Marcia.

"I have a counterproposal," said Steve. "Suppose we all return to the inn for a good night's sleep. We know

Ishihara can't allow any harm to come to Jane. Then tomorrow we can go on to the Great Wall to find the Polo family."

"I can't *believe* this," Marcia wailed. "You're just going to *forget* about her?"

"Of course not!" Steve snapped. "But Jane is just as safe with Ishihara as she would be with Hunter."

"That may not be precisely true," said Hunter. "Ishihara's judgment is in some doubt, since he is obviously following Wayne's instructions."

"You sure?" Steve asked. "As far as immediate harm to Jane goes, he can't let her get hurt. Just how much leeway do you robots have in your interpretations?"

Steve doubted he could change Hunter's mind about a First Law interpretation, but he wanted to try. He trusted Ishihara to keep Jane safe. The team could save a lot of time.

"Well, Hunter?"

"I cannot go on without Jane," said Hunter. "I agree that Ishihara would protect her from clear and immediate harm, but his judgment is in doubt regarding more complex situations. Further, I still remain responsible for Jane as part of my team. Also, if we can apprehend Wayne or even just Ishihara, we can eliminate further interference from them. That will make the rest of this mission and all of the next one much easier for us. I must pursue them and free Jane."

"Then we should split up," said Steve. "I don't know how many times I've suggested it already, but this time I'm really serious. You go after Jane, and Marcia and I can return to the inn for some sleep. Tomorrow we'll go north for the Polos. When you have Jane, come after us."

"As you know, I consider dividing the team to be a mistake."

"You let Jane and me sail back to Jamaica on a pirate ship without you. This is a much safer environment. Our real trouble seems to have been instigated by Wayne, not the local situation. Even the people who grabbed you and Jane would never have acted without Wayne."

Hunter turned to observe Marcia. "You are very cold and tired, are you not?"

"I'm afraid so," said Marcia. "And what he says makes some sense. Besides, you could probably help Jane a lot faster alone than you could with me along."

"And we'll blend into the crowd," Steve added. "Without you and Jane, we look like locals."

"The same people who kidnapped Jane and me have almost certainly returned to the inn. I cannot have them carry you two away. I suggest you take rooms at the other inn we saw."

"No need." Steve grinned. "Now that we know they think you're a spirit, we can manage them, I think. Anyhow, they've probably gone to bed. We'll be careful about going back inside. If we don't see them, we'll go upstairs."

"This is also a great danger," said Hunter. "At the very least, you should take a room at the other inn."

"Maybe not," said Marcia. "I think they focused on you and Jane in part because of your European appearance. And they were running pretty fast when they passed us on the road a while ago. Maybe they've had enough."

"We're wasting time," said Steve. "Every minute we debate, Jane is being taken farther south. But I also want to return to the same inn because of the innkeeper. He made a point to come and tell me that Jane had been taken."

"You feel safer with him?" Hunter asked.

"Yeah, you could put it that way," said Steve.

"I will return to the inn with you," said Hunter. "If it is quiet, and you can return to your rooms unseen, then I will allow us to separate. Clearly, you both need to stay warm and get some sleep."

Steve hiked back up the road with Hunter and Marcia, relieved that Hunter had given in. The mountain air had grown very sharp, and by the time they returned to the inn, he was even more ready than before for a warm bed. Hunter stepped up to the front door, preparing to open it.

"I should do it," Steve said quietly. "If those guests are awake, they may react to seeing you."

Hunter moved back to make room for Steve.

Steve found the front door of the inn barred. That was certainly normal for this hour. He rapped on it sharply.

"Who's there?" The innkeeper's voice was cautious and fearful, but clearly wide awake.

"Three of your guests," Steve called. "We are well. Please open."

He heard the bar slide to one side. The innkeeper opened the door a crack and glanced at them all before opening it wide and stepping back. He bowed to them repeatedly, expecting them to come right inside.

"Are your other guests awake?" Steve stayed where he was, with Hunter and Marcia behind him.

"Eh?" He gestured for them to enter.

"Your other guests, who took our woman friend. They came running back here, didn't they?"

"Oh, yes. They were all very excited about something

when they first came back. Now they have all gone to sleep up in their rooms."

"We would prefer not to be seen by them."

"Of course. Please come in. Your friend is not with you?" He glanced past Steve.

"No. But we are not blaming you. In the morning, we will remain in our rooms until you tell us they have left. Is this agreeable?"

"Of course."

Steve turned to Hunter. "I really think we'll be okay. In the morning, we'll stay in our rooms until he tells us the others have hit the road. They won't bother us."

"All right. But I am concerned that you will take unnecessary risks."

"There shouldn't be any risks," said Steve. "We'll just let the others get a head start on us in the morning. Then during the day we'll make sure we don't catch up."

"Is it okay?" Marcia asked. "I'd like to do this. I'm really cold."

"It is fine," said Hunter. "I will go prepare my horse. I will take Jane's, too."

"Good night," said Steve. He stepped aside for Marcia to enter first, as Hunter left for the stable.

"Night," Marcia muttered, yawning as she turned and went inside.

Steve followed her. Behind them, the innkeeper barred the door again.

Several minutes later, Hunter forced his weary horse into a canter; the the reins of Jane's mount were tied to his saddle. He was not comfortable with the further splitting of his team, but he could also see that Marcia badly needed rest. Even Steve, though he was more accustomed to physical activity than Marcia, would quickly become too tired to act efficiently unless he slept for the remainder of the night.

In the absence of a more pressing emergency, Hunter had to let them sleep in the relative comfort and safety of the inn. He accepted that Steve and Marcia would be reasonably secure at the inn as long as the other guests did not see them. He also trusted Steve to act wisely.

At the same time, he felt he had failed to take proper care of his team. Wayne had already succeeded in interrupting their search for MC 5. Now Hunter had to prevent him from taking full advantage of the situation.

As Hunter rode down the moonlit mountain road, he slowed the horses to a walk to preserve their energy. With his vision on maximum light receptivity, he identified the fresh tracks that matched the sounds he had heard earlier. The most recent donkey tracks leading south were much deeper than the same ones Xiao Li's animal had made riding north; the horse tracks with them were deep enough to have been made by the horse whose heavy hoofbeats he had heard.

Hunter had to plan his approach to his quarry. He chose not to radio Ishihara with any sort of threat or argument, since Wayne clearly had become more persuasive in making his case to Ishihara. Any such transmission would merely reveal to Ishihara that he was chasing them and give Ishihara some fix on the distance between them. Hunter's best chance to rescue Jane and apprehend Wayne would be to sneak up on them.

Hunter did not know if Ishihara's hearing ability was fully equal to his own. Since Hunter had been designed specifically to search for MC Governor, he had been given some abilities greater than most robots, but he had never specifically compared his hearing to Ishihara's. However, he was certain that Ishihara's aural sense was greater than any human's. That lessened his chance of making an unheard approach.

Obviously, Hunter's pursuit would become obvious if he simply cantered up behind them, since even Wayne would hear that. Hunter could, however, draw closer slowly. When he heard the first faint sounds of hoofbeats up ahead, he could pace them at a distance until he formed a specific plan.

If Ishihara's hearing equaled his own, however, then Ishihara might hear Hunter's horses at the same time. The question of stealth might in fact turn on uncontrollable variables, such as the direction of the wind or the echo pattern off the surrounding slopes. He would have to remain aware of those as he continued on his way.

Now that he had identified the tracks, however, he did not have to study each hoofprint carefully. He could see the trail plainly enough. Instead, he turned his attention to the condition of his mount. The tired animal kept slowing down, and had to be prodded forward.

After more than a mile, the tracks of his quarry still followed the road. Hunter had expected more effort at evasion, but postulated that Ishihara, under the First Law, could not take the risk of allowing the humans to flee through the mountains in the darkness. Another possibility was that Wayne had simply decided to forget about evasion. He might be taking his companions as far as they could go straight down the road before their mounts wore out.

Hunter still expected that the two mounts ahead of him would tire more quickly than his own. All of them had traveled a long way earlier in the day, but the mounts ahead of him were, by his calculation, carrying two riders each; one was merely a donkey, whose short legs had to take many more strides to keep up with the horse. Maybe they were gambling that Hunter's substantial weight would tire his horse first, instead.

He considered that possibility unlikely, but the burden on his horse was real. To minimize it, he moved to Jane's mount in order to rest his own. Wayne did not have that option.

In the lobby the innkeeper gave Steve a small brass oil lamp before sleepily returning to bed. Leading Marcia upstairs, Steve was relieved to find the corridor quiet. He turned to Marcia to say good night. She stopped at the door to her room, looking at him uncertainly in the shifting light.

"What's wrong?" Steve asked quietly. "Everybody else here is asleep. We'll be okay."

"I know," she said softly. "But . . ."

"What?" He could see that her arrogance had vanished. "What is it?"

"I was thinking about your other missions. Were they like this?"

"Like this? What do you mean?"

"Well, how dangerous were they? When you talk about buccaneers and dinosaurs and everything else, were you really in serious danger?"

"Yes. We were."

"I don't think the risk became real to me until Hunter was kidnapped."

Steve nodded. "I know. All of you who live in cities in our own time have robots around you constantly."

"Yes. I never even thought about it before because I was so used to it."

"I think we're in less danger now than usual. Hunter is between us and Wayne and Ishihara." He gestured toward the rooms around them. "We should keep quiet and just go to sleep, so we don't wake up the kidnappers."

Marcia nodded and opened the door to her room. "Of course. Sorry."

"Make sure you bar the door behind you," he added. "Light your candle with this." He carefully handed her the brass lamp and waited while she took it into her room. A moment later, she brought it back out, silhouetted by the candle flame flickering behind her on a small table.

"Good night." She yawned again and went into her room, closing the door behind her.

Steve waited in the hall until he heard her slide the bar into place. Then he went into his own room and did the same. In a few minutes, he was sound asleep.

As the hours passed, Hunter could feel Jane's mount tiring. Both horses walked more slowly. He changed mounts again, but his horse now had to be kicked more often to keep up the pace. The moon was about to set. His magnified vision revealed that the tracks ahead of him remained on the road. However, his hearing no longer detected the sound of hoofbeats ahead.

This puzzled him. Considering the amount of weight the mounts ahead of him had to carry, he had expected that he would either have drawn close enough to hear them by now, or else he would have seen the tracks leave the road for the forested hills. Since Hunter had already concluded that Ishihara would not take that risk at night, he was not surprised to see the tracks continue on the road, but he had apparently missed something.

Hunter reined in and dismounted. He kneeled to examine the tracks. Even his magnified vision needed help now that the moonlight had faded.

Carefully, he studied the depth of the tracks and then compared them to those of his own horses. He also saw that the hoofprints his own mount made now, shuffling wearily on the road, were much shallower than the ones just a few feet back, when Hunter had still been in the saddle. Suddenly he realized that the horse and donkey in front of him were no longer carrying the amount of weight they had been when he had begun tracking them. From the saddle, in the waning light, the difference in the appearance of the hoofprints had been too slight for him to see, but it was clear now.

Somehow, those he was following had dismounted and left the road without leaving footprints. Hunter had been fooled, most likely by Ishihara lifting Wayne and Jane directly from their mounts into the trees. He had also miscalculated Ishihara's interpretation of the danger that the forested hills would offer to his human companions at night.

That triggered his own First Law concern. If Ishihara's judgment was questionable, then Hunter could not conclude that the humans with him were safe, as he had believed to this point. He hoped they were hiding in one spot, maybe for the humans to rest. That would be less dangerous than hiking through the mountains.

Hunter concluded that Xiao Li was probably riding the horse now and leading the donkey. His weight was slight enough not to alter these hoofprints significantly. Certainly the tired animals would not have continued down the road all night on their own. At least one rider had to be urging them forward.

Now Hunter had to decide how to investigate all these surmises. He had two essential problems: the near-exhaustion of both his horses and the deepening darkness. Both problems could be improved by waiting several hours.

Once his horses had rested, even for a short time, they would move a little faster. Daylight would allow him to follow tracks even in the forest. Now that Wayne, Ishihara, and Jane were on foot, he would have the advantage.

Hunter hobbled his horses and sat down by the side of the road to conserve his energy and wait for dawn.

Jane waited in the forest with Wayne and Ishihara. Neither of them insisted on holding her every moment. All three of them knew that she could not outrun Ishihara, so she did not bother trying.

A short time earlier, at Wayne's suggestion, Ishihara had lifted Wayne and Jane from their mounts to sturdy branches of trees near the road. Then he had followed them. Once they had all jumped to the ground on the far side of the trees, in the darkness away from the road, they waited for Wayne to decide what to do next.

Meanwhile, Xiao Li had ridden on down the road with their mounts. Ishihara had allowed this because he knew that Hunter would not harm the boy. Since Xiao Li had followed them up here on his own, Ishihara felt he would be safe on this road a little longer.

"We can't fool Hunter for long," Wayne said. His voice was strained and anxious.

"What do you suggest?" Ishihara asked.

"Well . . . I don't know. But our mounts were about to fall over from fatigue. We had to do something. And if Hunter grabs me, my hopes are finished."

"You really don't have that much to worry about," said Jane. "I still think the Oversight Committee will handle their review of your robots responsibly."

"Don't bother; I've heard it before." Wayne looked at Ishihara. "You have any ideas?"

"I have one."

"Yeah? What is it?"

"We can use the time travel unit to move all the way forward to Khanbaliq, arriving tomorrow morning. Since we know Hunter is behind us, and has no lead on MC 5, Hunter cannot gain on us during the period we are skipping."

"Say . . . that's right." Wayne nodded. "Before, I was always worried that Hunter would take the component robot during the interval we were jumping. This time we know where he is. And we'll have the advantage."

"What about Xiao Li?" Jane asked suddenly.

"What about him?" Wayne shrugged. "He'll be all right. This is his time."

"Ishihara, he's just a child. And he's only riding around the mountains in the middle of the night because of you two. How can you just abandon him?"

"I expect Hunter to catch him and protect him. With that likelihood established, my first duty is to you two, as humans from our time."

"But you don't *know* he's safe," said Jane, wishing she had thought of this argument earlier.

"Hunter is tracking him," said Ishihara.

"We'll go back to the outskirts of Khanbaliq," Wayne said firmly. "We'll arrive tomorrow morning, back out by the village. Since they've already seen us appear like magic, we can do it again."

"They'll ask about Xiao Li," said Jane. "What are you going to tell them?"

"That he'll be fine," said Wayne. "Besides, we didn't bring him with us; he came on his own. He can find his way home if he has to."

"That's very callous," said Jane.

"Let's go now," said Wayne, ignoring her.

"All right," said Ishihara.

Steve slept late the next morning. Even when he woke up, he lay in bed listening to the sounds elsewhere in the inn. He heard doors opening and closing on his corridor; downstairs, footsteps clunked and a chair scraped on the floor, accompanied by muffled conversation.

None of the voices sounded excited. He had not heard Marcia's door open. Quietly, in no hurry, he got up and dressed.

As the morning passed, Steve finally heard the other guests go outside one by one. Soon the clopping of horses' hooves reached him as the other patrons rode away. Then a lone set of footsteps walked up the stairs and down the hall.

"Sir?" The innkeeper rapped quietly. "The other guests have taken their leave now."

Steve opened the door. "Thank you. I'll get my wife. We will have two breakfasts."

"Of course." With a quick bow, he hurried away.

Marcia opened her door, already dressed. "I've been listening. Everything's okay, huh?"

"Yeah," said Steve. "You okay?"

"Basically. I'm sore from all that riding yesterday." She winced as she walked out into the hall.

"I'm afraid we have more of the same today. But before we go downstairs, I want to call Hunter."

"All right."

"Hunter, Steve and Marcia here. How are you?"

"I am well but have had no success. How are you two? And where are you?" Hunter's voice was faint and almost drowned out by a great deal of static.

"We just got up at the inn. The other guests have left, so we're okay. Where are you?"

"I am down the road but on my way back toward you," said Hunter. "I waited for dawn to rest my horse and to have more light."

"You're coming back?" Marcia asked. "That's great, but what happened to Jane?"

"Ishihara fooled me in the darkness. I followed the tracks of Xiao Li and the animals long after the others had left the road for the forest."

"What did they do?"

"They moved to the trees directly from their mounts. It is a move familiar to me from our missions to the Late Cretaceous and to Roman Germany, but in the darkness I failed to spot the location."

"Where's Xiao Li now?" Marcia asked. "Did you catch up to him?"

"No. I backtracked at sunrise."

"Is he going to be okay?" Steve asked.

"I believe so," said Hunter. "My first duty is to Jane, in any case; it must take precedence over my First Law concern over a local human."

"Are you sure?" Marcia asked.

"Yes."

"So what happened?" Steve asked.

"Not much," said Hunter. "I had to examine the tracks closely in order to see where they suddenly became shallower, indicating less weight. Eventually, I was able to find the area where the others had moved into the trees."

"Why aren't you still following them?" Steve was puzzled. "You wouldn't just give up."

"A short distance from the road, all the tracks and marks in the trees and brush vanish."

"That's impossible," said Marcia. Then her tone changed. "Uh, isn't it?"

"No," said Hunter. "After carefully reviewing my observations, I can only conclude that Wayne took Jane and Ishihara to another time."

"Oh, no," Steve muttered.

"They *left?*" Marcia stared at Steve in horror. "Now what do we do?"

"Ishihara still has to protect Jane," Steve reminded her calmly, "no matter where they went."

"But where are they?"

"Theoretically, they could be anywhere in history and geography," said Hunter.

"What do you think they would do?" Steve asked. He was more worried than he wanted to reveal to Marcia.

"Wayne still wants to capture MC 5," said Hunter. "They have probably gone right back to Khanbaliq."

"You said you're coming back toward us," said Steve. "Why don't you go back to Khanbaliq after them? We'll go on to the Great Wall to find the Polos. After we learn if they can help us with MC 5, we'll rejoin you in a day or two."

"I dare not. Because of losing Jane, I am again suffering from a feeling of failure. I must reunite with you two as soon as I can."

"Well, we're still going to have breakfast, but . . . how far are you?" Steve asked. "If we sit here and wait, we'll lose a lot of time."

"I estimate that I am roughly half a day's ride behind you at this moment."

"You'll catch up some while we're eating. Then I think we should go on north. We're safe enough. You'll catch up to us tonight."

"Probably," said Hunter. "Now that the sun is replenishing my energy, I can jog alongside the horses I have with me. That will relieve them of the burden of my weight. However, they are still very tired."

"We'll be okay," said Steve.

"I can accept this if you can assure me you will call at the first sign of danger so we can discuss it," said Hunter. "And avoid all risks you can see."

"Of course," said Steve.

"Hunter out."

Steve and Marcia went downstairs. The innkeeper hurried out with their breakfast of rice gruel with meat and vegetables in it, and a pot of hot tea. He retired as Steve and Marcia started eating hungrily.

When Steve had finally satisfied himself, he leaned back with a grin and sipped a little more tea. "That sure is familiar. It's the same breakfast I've had in Chinese restaurants in our own time."

"That's true," said Marcia. "I recognize it, too. In fact, much of the Chinese cooking in our own time is, at least in style, many centuries old. Even new ingredients, such as corn from the New World, have been available since the Age of Exploration. An excavation on the Old Silk Road in the late twentieth century revealed mummified dumplings virtually identical to what we eat now. . . ."

Steve grinned as she prattled on with another of her lectures. After seeing her genuinely scared and vulnerable last night, this lecture did not annoy him the way the earlier ones had. Now it just struck him as funny. While she talked, Steve ordered some meat-filled buns they could take with them on the road.

When Marcia finished her lecture, even the tea was gone. Steve got the duffel bag out of his room and paid the innkeeper. Then he and Marcia walked out to the stable and had the hostler saddle their horses, which had already been fed. Steve paid him, too, and mounted up.

Marcia grimaced as she swung into the saddle. "I don't think I've ever used these muscles before. Not in this combination. It's not like riding a bike or a motorcycle at all."

"No." Steve grinned. "That's true." He kicked his mount and turned up the road.

Marcia steered her horse after him. "Well, it's a nice, clear, cool morning, isn't it?"

"Yes, it is. And we have a leisurely ride ahead. We don't dare catch up to the travelers ahead of us, and we want Hunter to catch up to us if he can."

"Good," said Marcia, with a wry grin. "Slow and easy sounds just fine to me."

Jane, Wayne, and Ishihara landed in early morning right outside a small peasant village. Several chickens and a couple of children darted away in surprise. Beyond the buildings of the village, Jane could see adults walking from the village into the fields with their farm tools.

As they got to their feet, Jane looked around in all directions. They were out of the mountains. Then she recognized the walls and towers of Khanbaliq a short distance away. In fact, she could see that they were fairly near the spot where Hunter had first brought his team from their own time.

She yawned and wondered if she would be able to sleep soon. Wayne also needed rest. She waited to see what her captors would do next.

An elderly man walked out of the house in the front of the village with an expression of concern on his face. He spoke sharply to the children, then stopped abruptly when he saw Wayne and Ishihara. The man bowed deeply to both of them.

Wayne and Ishihara responded in kind. Then Wayne leaned close to Ishihara and whispered something too low for Jane to hear. In turn, Ishihara spoke quietly to the elderly man, who nodded as he listened.

"Come on in," Wayne said to her in a casual tone. "We'll get some rest."

Their host took them inside to a small room. It had two sleeping pallets of straw, covered with some sort of rough cloth. The single window was shuttered.

"Thank you, Lao Li," Ishihara said to the villager, who bowed and left them alone.

"You and I both need a good night's sleep." Wayne looked pointedly at Jane. "Ishihara will remain with us both for safety and to make sure you stay with us."

"I'm too tired to run off," said Jane. She sat down on one of the pallets. "I guess this will do." Then she looked up at Ishihara. "Just make sure you stay here. I don't want to be left alone with him or in this village without you."

"No harm will come to either of you," said Ishihara.

Steve and Marcia rode slowly along the winding mountain road. Each time they crested a rise, he looked ahead for the travelers who had kidnapped Hunter and Jane the night before. Usually, they were too far ahead to see, but twice, when the terrain allowed him a particularly long view of the road ahead, he glimpsed the knot of riders moving north in the distance.

Several times during the day, Steve called Hunter just to make contact with him as he followed them. Frequently, Steve stopped to allow Marcia some time to dismount and walk around; that was all they could do about her stiff muscles. They ate the food he had brought from the inn and kept on riding.

Late in the day, they rode in the shadow of a mountain as they came around a curve. Below them, in a narrow pass between two steep mountainsides, sunlight angled across a huge gate in a massive gray wall. The wall had a rock base and high brick sides with crenellations across the top. A small town had grown up just inside the gate. Startled, Steve reined in to take a look.

Steve had seen pictures of the Great Wall of China, always long shots in which the wall snaked over the top of a ridge. Those distant shots had no reference by which a viewer could judge the size of the construction. Now, seeing the wall in front of him at a distance he could judge for himself, Steve simply stared at it.

"*Chuyungguan*," said Marcia. "That's the name of this gate. I was able to visit it once in our time. The version standing now was restored in the twentieth century, but it looked the same as this one to me."

Steve could see that this gate was in an important place. The arched gate ran under a watchtower, and high on each mountain to the east and west, another tower stood guard over the land. The narrow pass would be easy to defend, blocked by the Great Wall.

"How big *is* this thing?" Steve asked quietly. "How high are those towers?"

"The towers are about twelve meters high. They're about twelve meters square at the base and angle inward as they go up to about nine meters square at the top."

" 'About'?"

"They didn't use the metric system back then. They had a measurement system of their own. I'm rounding off the fractions."

Steve nodded, still gazing at it. "How high is the wall itself between the towers?"

"It varies. No shorter than about six meters and no higher than just over seven meters."

"That thing is thick, too, isn't it?"

"Just over seven and a half meters."

"Is it solid rock? Or brick?"

"Neither. They raised the inner and outer faces of stone and brick first, then filled the space between them with earth or clay. They pounded it down and then paved a brick road over the top of the wall."

"So they can march troops along the top."

"Yes. Or ride four horses side by side." She pointed to the three towers in turn. "They were placed within two bow shots of each other and they extend forward from the outer surface of the wall. The idea was that archers in the towers could reach attackers all along the front of the wall."

"I'm impressed."

"So were the Mongols." Marcia smiled. "Genghis Khan failed in a couple of assaults on this gate. He finally took it when another Mongol army under a subordinate broke through another gate that was less well defended and came up behind the Chinese defenders here."

"I guess no one needs it now, right? Kublai Khan rules on both sides of the wall."

"That's right. This gate has a small garrison, but in this time, it's more of a checkpoint for travelers than anything."

"Shall we ride on down? I guess the Polos will be down there somewhere."

"Sure."

Steve enjoyed the view as they rode down the slope into the narrow pass. As they descended, the wall loomed larger and higher than ever, a magnificent edifice that seemed to be part of the mountain ridge on which it had been built. As they drew closer they could see that the individual stones in the wall were very large. When Steve remembered the wall had been built entirely by human and animal labor, with no modern machinery or robots at all, it seemed even more impressive. Dusk had arrived by the time they reached the town just before the gate.

On the watchtower over the gate, and along the top of the wall, soldiers were silhouetted against the sky, all of them looking away to the north.

Steve could see that the gate was standing open. Four uniformed soldiers stood guard inside the gateway, leaning casually on their spears and looking attentively at something beyond his sight on the far side of the gate. At the sound of hoofbeats as Steve and Marcia drew near, the guards glanced idly back over their shoulders, then resumed looking through the gateway.

"What are they looking at?" Steve asked. He could hear the shouts of men and the thunder of many hooves in the distance. "Sounds like a lot of riders. Whatever it is, the sentries don't seem to be alarmed by it."

"I have no idea."

"Let's go see."

"I don't think that's such a good idea." Marcia shook her head vigorously. "No."

"Come on, why not? You've been here before, but I haven't. I want to see the wall up close. Do you think we can go up in one of the towers?"

"No!"

"What's wrong?"

"Look, it's a tourist attraction only in *our* time," Marcia said anxiously. "I wouldn't ask these soldiers just to show us around."

"Why not?"

"To use a modern phrase, this is a functioning military installation, even if it's not as important now as it used to be." Marcia lapsed into her lecturing tone again. "And we aren't Mongols; they see the Chinese as a conquered people. Asking to go up in the tower could raise the suspicion that we might attempt sabotage or espionage in some form."

"Even an ordinary couple like us?"

"As soon as we ask to tour the watchtower, we won't be ordinary anymore. We'll look very odd. Like I said, this is not a place for tourists in this time."

"Well ... I see."

"Good."

"But we can still go find out what they're looking at. I mean, the gate's standing wide open."

"I don't think we should."

"Well, look, we have to ask someone about the Polos

anyway. They should know. Come on." Steve kicked his mount and rode up to the gate.

"Well, *be careful*." Shaking her head, Marcia followed him reluctantly.

"Should we speak Mongol to them?"

"No. Judging by their armor and their weapons, they're Chinese."

"They are?"

"Even under the khan, the Mongol armies and the Chinese armies are distinct."

"Why don't they have just the Mongol army now, if the khan is worried about the Chinese rebelling?"

"The Mongol army alone isn't big enough to garrison the whole Chinese empire. The khan needs the Chinese army for that. The Chinese army is controlled by generals put in place by the khan, as Emperor of China."

"Oh. Well, okay. I get the idea." Steve felt that if he was polite and careful, he could at least see what had caught the attention of the sentries. Besides, if the Polos had passed through the gate, the sentries were the ones to ask.

As he reined in at the gate, the sentries turned to look up at him. All four were stocky, muscular young men. They seemed more resigned than wary.

"What is your business here?" One sentry, marginally taller than the others, straightened up.

"I have heard that the Polo family took this road in the last day or so," said Steve. "Marco Polo and his father and uncle. I seek them."

The other three guards also drew themselves up, suddenly interested. The Polo name obviously carried some importance. However, all four sentries looked at each other and shook their heads.

"They have not come this way recently," said the first

sentry politely. "We know their name, because they are favored by the Emperor. We have seen them on this road in past years, but not recently."

Steve was startled, but he nodded courteously. He suddenly realized that Xiao Li's story had been a falsehood from beginning to end. As soon as he could report to Hunter without local witnesses, he would.

Behind him, Marcia sighed audibly.

Steve pointed through the open gateway. Several large groups of men were riding in the distance, across patches of rugged, steeply sloped steppe surrounded by forest. "Who are they? What are they doing?"

The sentry frowned. "A local Mongol battalion has camped just outside the wall. They are practicing maneuvers, no more. After all, we are many miles from the borders of the Emperor's empire here."

"Really?" Apparently more comfortable now, Marcia rode up closer to Steve and looked out, too.

Steve could see hundreds of riders moving together in one group, their banners flying on upright lances. In the distance behind them, a separate group was wheeling about, riding through a sharp turn. A third group of riders stood on a far hill, unmoving.

"That looks like fun," said Steve.

"Don't you dare," Marcia whispered loudly.

"Calm down." He grinned. "I'm not going out there. But I used to ride out in the Mojave Desert. My favorite horse was a half–quarter horse, half-Arabian mare."

"These are Mongol horses."

"I know. Arabians have more delicate features and more high-strung temperaments. But both are small, hardy desert breeds."

"You still have your horse?" She looked at him with a new curiosity.

"No. I don't have any of them now. But I miss that one the most." He nodded to the sentries and reined his mount around. "Come on."

Steve rode a short distance away from the sentries and all the small buildings in the little settlement. Marcia followed him. When he was out of the hearing of everyone else, he leaned close to Marcia.

"We'll pretend we're talking to each other, since people can see us. I'm calling Hunter."

"All right."

"Hunter, Steve here."

For once, Hunter did not answer.

"Hunter, you there?"

Marcia's eyes widened as she looked at Steve.

"Hunter?"

Only static hissed quietly from the lapel pin.

"Maybe my transmitter's broken," said Steve. "Try calling him on yours."

Marcia switched on her pin. "Hunter? Marcia calling. Steve and I have reached the Great Wall."

She, too, received only static and shut it off. "What do you think happened?"

Steve turned to look back the way they had come. "Maybe nothing. He was about a half day's ride behind us, and we've come through some very rugged country, much rougher than the ground we covered yesterday. The mountains block radio signals. He's probably still coming."

"Then why could we communicate last night?"

"It depends on the configuration of the mountains and passes. The signal can bounce, too. It's impossible to predict exactly where it will go."

"Then you think he's still coming?"

"Yeah."

"So what are we going to do?"

Steve looked at the sky. The sun had gone behind the mountains, and the sky was reddening with sunset. The air had abruptly chilled even in the brief time since they had arrived at the gate.

Marcia waited, looking back up the road as though she hoped to see Hunter.

"Well, I guess we wasted a lot of time coming here," said Steve.

"You think the Polos turned off the road somewhere along the way?"

"No," said Steve. "If you remember, we haven't passed any forks today."

"I saw some paths. Hunting trails, most likely. These mountains provide game for the emperors."

"I don't think the Polos came this way at all. Xiao Li must have pulled a fast one from the very start. I should have figured that out last night, but so much was going on, I never thought it all through."

"None of us did, with Jane and Hunter being carried off," said Marcia. "But, as I asked you a moment ago, what are we going to do?"

"I guess we can take a room—two if you prefer— for the night. Hunter should arrive sometime later. Tomorrow, we can go back to Khanbaliq."

"Oh, no. Some of the same people must be here in one of the inns—the people who kidnapped Hunter and Jane."

"Well . . . that's true." Steve looked around. The little town had three inns with stables, some small houses, and seven taverns. "This is a strange place."

"Yes, it's just a road stop, really. Travelers would account for the number of inns, of course. But only the garrison of guards on the Great Wall could support that many taverns in a settlement this size."

"Do they live in the houses?"

"No. They're garrisoned in the towers along the wall. The houses must be owned by some well-to-do tavern owners or innkeepers who can live separately from their businesses." She shrugged. "Hard to tell, really."

"Look, that group of travelers stayed together all day. At least, every time I saw them, they were still together. If they've taken rooms in the same inn, then we have two others where we can stay."

"But they might have split up. Besides, how are we going to know where they are?"

"Come on."

Steve reined his horse back around and rode to the nearest inn, where he stopped with Marcia outside the stable. Most of the horses were out of sight, but the hostler was grooming one. Steve had been hoping to recognize the horses belonging to the other group, but he had not taken any special notice of them yesterday.

"I'm going to look inside the inn," said Steve. "Stay on your horse, all right?"

"All right."

Steve dismounted and quietly walked up onto the front porch of the small wooden building. He opened the door and leaned inside, looking around. It was much like the inn in which they had stayed the night before, with a large room full of tables in front of a big fireplace. The furniture was more finely finished, carved and deeply polished, suggesting greater prosperity. Long, vertical landscape paintings hung on the walls.

"Welcome, friend." A big, burly innkeeper hurried forward, smiling.

Past him, Steve recognized a couple of merchants from the group he wanted to avoid.

"Sorry," Steve muttered quickly. He pulled out of the doorway and closed the door quickly behind him. From what he could tell, no one except the innkeeper had seen him.

"What happened?" Marcia asked.

"They're in there," said Steve, as he swung into the saddle. "That's good, because now we know where they are. I don't think anyone saw me."

"Then we can stay at another inn."

"I'll do the same thing again, in case that group had to split up to get rooms."

They rode to another inn. Again, Marcia waited outside. Steve looked inside this one and did not recognize any of the visitors who had sat down to dinner. He stepped inside, still looking around cautiously.

This time a slender, white-haired man approached him and bowed. "Good evening, stranger. Are you in need of lodging?"

"I may be," said Steve. "I, uh, had an argument yesterday with other travelers along this road. I would like to avoid them if I can."

"I see. Well, I have some soldiers here on their way south to Khanbaliq."

"The ones I'm talking about are going north. Some merchants and students, as well as soldiers."

"I have no group like that."

Steve grinned with relief. "Good. Uh, I have a companion. We'll take two rooms. And two dinners."

"Very well. I ask six coppers for each room."

"Fine. I'll take our horses to the stable."

"Of course."

As Steve hurried out, he realized that he had forgotten to bargain. It was too late now; he had revealed to the innkeeper that he had reason to avoid the other inns, which had ruined his bargaining position. He decided not to worry about it. In this case, a safe place to wait for Hunter was more important than exactly how much they spent.

The hostler was a tall, gaunt man with graying hair who walked stiffly with age. With a weary, uninterested nod, he took the reins from Steve and Marcia. Steve untied the cloth bag with their changes of clothes from the back of the saddle. As they started toward the inn, hoofbeats came through the gate and they turned to look.

A group of Mongol riders rode through the gate. Grinning, they arrogantly ignored the Chinese sentries who glared sullenly at them, and split up. Small knots of riders trotted toward different taverns and inns. Four young riders, dressed in furs with breastplates, backplates, and pointed steel caps, came toward Steve and Marcia.

"I guess the battalion was dismissed," said Steve.

"Let's get inside," said Marcia. "I'm scared."

"All right."

They turned away.

"Ho! You there!" One of the soldiers called out in accented Chinese.

"Ignore him," Marcia whispered. "Let's just get inside."

"I better not," said Steve. "We don't want to make them mad." He turned and looked up at the riders. "Good evening," he said in Mongol.

The lead rider raised his eyebrows in surprise. "You speak our language?"

"Yes, friend. And I see you have fine horses. We saw

you ride a few minutes ago, beyond the wall." Steve figured a compliment would always be wise.

"The best in Mongolia." The rider grinned, seeming to mock his own boasting. "You know horses?"

"A little," Steve said modestly. He was certain that boasting himself would be a mistake. "I had a very fine one of a different desert breed once. She was the kind ridden by the Arabs."

"Ah! My uncle rode against the Arabs in the west. He fought in Persia."

"Then he must have seen the same breed."

"He must have." The Mongol shrugged. "Is this inn crowded? We seek Chinese wine. I prefer it to our koumiss."

"Uh, no, it's not crowded."

"Good." He swung out of the saddle, and his companions did likewise. Without even looking at the hostler, he gestured for the old man to take their horses. He turned to Steve. "You will come and drink with us as my guest."

"Well, I have ordered dinner for my friend and me," said Steve uncertainly.

"Do what he says," Marcia muttered quickly in English. "Keep him happy. But they know a decent woman won't drink with them, so I'm going up to my room. Bring me something to eat when you can, okay?" She took the cloth bag from him.

"All right," said Steve. He didn't know what else to do. "But what's koumiss?"

"Fermented mare's milk." Marcia hurried into the inn ahead of them.

Steve grimaced at the idea of that, then turned to the Mongol leader, speaking in Mongol again. "Thank you. I will be honored to join you."

The Mongol clapped him on the shoulder. "Wine and food for all of us," he called to the innkeeper in his accented Chinese. "Your best."

The innkeeper bowed deeply and rushed away.

The Mongol leader led the group to the table closest to the fireplace and gestured for them all to sit down.

Steve sat down with the Mongols, smiling at each one with a nod of greeting. When he got the chance, he would ask the innkeeper to take Marcia's dinner up to her. Right now, he felt it was wise not to remind the Mongols that she was up there.

"What is your name?" The Mongol pointed to himself. "I am Timur."

"Steve."

"Ss—teve. The sound is unusual to me. But of course, my Chinese is not so good."

The other Mongols introduced themselves in turn, but Steve could not understand the unfamiliar names he heard. He decided not to ask that they repeat them. Instead, he simply nodded again courteously.

"So, you must be a rider," said Timur.

"Not like you are. I saw you from the gate, riding on maneuvers. I could never ride that well."

"I am curious about you, Steve. I never met a Chinese man who had bothered to learn our language before. Tell us more about this other breed of horse."

"Uh, well, the Arabians were bred to the southern

deserts, at low altitude, near the sea." Steve was no expert on the history of Arabians, so he dropped that approach. "My best horse had a sharp, delicate nose and a small body. She was very hardy. I remember, she never even seemed to notice if the wind was blowing up a sandstorm or if it was raining. All weather was the same to her."

"A sandstorm?" Timur asked. "You rode her in the desert, then?"

"Well, yes."

"This must have been the same time when you learned our language, eh?"

"Yes, it was." Steve hesitated, glad to see the innkeeper come hurrying out with a piece of candle and wine and wine cups. A younger man followed him with bowls of noodles and strips of meat. Steve did not want to be drawn into questions about how he had learned to speak Mongol. As soon as the innkeeper had lit the candle and poured wine for them all, Steve lifted a cup. "I toast my new friends."

"Ah!" Timur grinned and held up his own. His friends joined in and they all drank.

Before Timur could ask more questions about Steve's experience among Mongols in the desert, Steve turned to one of the other Mongols. "Tell me about your experiences in the battalion. Have you fought anyone recently?"

"No, I have not had the chance." The man shook his head as he started eating.

"We are too young, all of us," said Timur. "We missed the great wars of conquest by the khakhan, which were finished before we came of age."

"But we are ready," said another, "and eager for the chance. We must prove ourselves every day and hope that our battalion will be sent to a distant land someday."

"It would be very exciting," Steve said carefully, as he began eating his own dinner. He tried to think of another question that would keep the conversation away from his own life. "You're off duty tonight? Why isn't the whole battalion coming to drink? Only a few of you came through the gate."

Timur laughed. "No, no, you don't understand. Those of us who came through the gate all have sentry duty tonight, to begin when the torches are doused and the camp sleeps. We have some free time before then."

"I see."

The Mongols ate and drank eagerly, without speaking further. Steve decided he could take the time to eat his own dinner. Timur's curiosity about him seemed satisfied.

Everyone finished eating without more comment. Steve hoped he could take some food up to Marcia soon, but that would have to wait until the Mongols had left. However, Timur leaned back with another cup of wine and looked up at Steve.

"Which tribe did you ride with?" Timur asked.

Steve froze. He thought he remembered Marcia mentioning something about Mongol tribes, but he could not recall what she had said. Maybe he was mistaken about that.

"What's wrong?" Timur studied his face.

"I, uh, rode with friends. That's all."

"Friends? But you must have lived on the grasslands, didn't you? If you rode out in the desert at times."

"I was a loner."

Timur shrugged. "About these Arabian horses. Can they carry a man day and night, across deserts and mountains? When we are on the march, we push our horses to the point of dropping, but they carry us where they must."

Steve almost asked him how he would know, since he had never been to war, but he knew better. It would only anger them. "I am sure you have the finest horses in the world. Everyone knows that."

Timur nodded, and drained his wine cup. "We must return to the camp to begin sentry duty." He glanced at his companions. "And no mention of how much Chinese wine we have drunk, eh?" He grinned at Steve. "The punishment for falling asleep on watch is death."

Steve wasn't sure how to respond to that, so he said nothing. When the Mongols rose from their chairs, he did, too. Timur tossed some coins to the innkeeper.

"Farewell on your travels, Steve. Show us one of those horses one day if you can—or maybe we'll ride to Arabia and see them for ourselves!" He laughed and led his companions out of the inn.

"Farewell," Steve called after them.

When they had gone, he drew in a deep breath and let it out. He only realized now how tense he had been throughout the dinner, concentrating on his company to avoid offending them. Now just beginning to relax, he turned to the innkeeper, who was clearing the table.

"Bring out dinner for my friend," Steve said in Chinese, picking up the candle from the table. "I'll go up and ask her to come down."

"Very well. I showed her to the first two rooms on the left." The innkeeper hustled away with an armload of dirty dishes and cups.

Steve grinned slightly as he climbed the stairs to the second floor by the flickering light of the small candle he carried. He was sure Marcia would be amused by the story of his dinner with the Mongols. Since he had managed to avoid angering them, and had somehow survived the question of how he could speak Mongol, it would make a funny anecdote.

He rapped lightly on the door of one of the two rooms they had taken.

"Marcia? Steve. The Mongols have left. You can come downstairs for dinner now."

When he received no answer, he knocked on the door of the other room. "Marcia? You awake?" After a pause, he tried the door, expecting it to be barred. Instead, it was open. The room was empty.

He moved back to the other room and tried the door. Also unbarred, it swung open easily. The cloth bag Steve had carried on his horse with their changes of clothes lay on the bed. Marcia was not here, either.

Worried, he looked down to the far end of the corridor. To his right, another staircase led down. He walked down the hall for a better look. Down the stairs, he could see one doorway that led down the corridor on the ground floor and another that led outside. Maybe she had just gone out to the latrine and had taken the back stairs to avoid passing the Mongols.

Steve decided he would wait for a minute to see if she returned. It was time to try calling Hunter again, anyway. He walked back to the room and switched on his lapel pin. Before he could speak, however, he heard the hoofbeats of several horses coming through it.

Alarmed, he listened carefully. The hoofbeats were cantering, too many for him to hear how many horses were present. The sound was clear, with minimal static, meaning that Marcia's lapel pin was still nearby. No one spoke. However, he knew what it meant; like Jane when she had been kidnapped, Marcia had managed to turn on her lapel pin so it could transmit whatever sounds occurred around her.

Some people had kidnapped Marcia, apparently by using the back stairs and the rear entrance.

Hunter would also be listening to it, wherever he was. However, with Marcia's lapel pin switched on, Steve could not call Hunter without being heard by the people who had taken Marcia. Steve could only assume they were the same group he had seen at the other inn, who had kidnapped Hunter and Jane. He had mistakenly believed that when he had stuck his head in the door and seen a couple of them that they had not seen him.

Exactly why they had taken Marcia remained a mystery, but it did not matter right now. He grabbed the cloth bag and hurried back downstairs. At the sound of his feet pounding on the steps, the innkeeper rushed around the corner to find him.

"Something wrong?" The innkeeper asked.

"My friend is gone. Who came in the back door while I was having dinner? Did you see them?"

"No. I heard some people come in, but I have other guests here. I thought they had gone out to the latrine and come back. I did not look to see who they were."

"Yeah, all right. Hold her dinner. And our rooms. I expect to be back." Steve strode out the front door into the chilly mountain air again.

A single paper lantern swung in the breeze over the stable. Under it, the tall, gaunt hostler sat on a wooden chest, bundled in fur robes. He took a swig of something from a narrow earthenware bottle.

"Saddle my horse, please," Steve said.

At the sound of his voice, the hostler jerked in surprise. His eyes widened fearfully as he recognized Steve in the moonlight. He said nothing.

"Come on. I'm in a hurry." Steve reached into his leather pouch for a couple of small coins and started to toss them to the old man. Then he saw that the hostler had made no move to catch them.

"What's wrong?" Steve asked. "I need my horse."

The man just stared at him, quivering.

"What is it?"

The old man tightened the fur robes around him.

"Look—did you see some people leave by the back door a little while ago with my friend?"

The man still just looked at him. Over his head, the paper lantern swayed gently. Finally, as Steve glared at him, he nodded slightly.

Steve remembered turning over the reins of their horses to him when they had arrived. At the time, the hostler had acted as though doing his job was just a tiresome chore. He had shown no interest in Steve or Marcia personally at all.

"Tell me what happened," Steve demanded angrily, stepping forward. "I want to know where my friend went."

The terrified old man shook his head, dropping the earthenware bottle slowly to the ground with a thud.

"Did someone speak to you? Tell me what happened!" Steve shouted.

The hostler was scared beyond the ability to speak. Shadows shifted across his face as the lantern swung back and forth. He stared at Steve, motionless.

Steve fought to control his anger. He took a deep breath and stepped back. Shouting would not get him anywhere. He could saddle his own horse, of course, but now he had to know what had scared the hostler.

"Why are you scared of me? I won't hurt you." Steve took several more coins out of his pouch. Holding them in this open palm, he slowly walked toward the man and dropped the coins on his lap. Then he backed away again. "Did someone tell you I would hurt you?"

The old man looked down at the money, then up at Steve again. Slowly, he moved one hand to cover the coins. Then he eyed Steve again.

"I won't hurt you," Steve said gently. "I just want to find my friend."

The old hostler studied his face for a moment, then looked around in the darkness nearby. He swallowed and picked up the coins in one hand. Then he fumbled around for his earthenware bottle.

Steve stepped forward and picked it up. He brushed off some bits of dirt and broken straw and handed it to the old man. Then he moved away again.

The hostler took a long drink. He lowered the bottle, wincing, and let out a long breath. He looked up at Steve again, less frightened than before.

"What happened to my friend?" Steve asked.

"You act like an ordinary man."

"Yeah, I guess. Why wouldn't I?"

"They told me you deal with evil spirits," he muttered, looking away.

"What? Who told you?"

"Some men from another inn," he said quietly. "They said you and your woman deal with evil spirits."

"Look, it's not true. We don't deal with evil spirits. It's a misunderstanding."

"They seemed so sure. And some of them are educated young men."

"It's not their fault." Steve struggled to hide his

impatience. "Another man has fooled them. But I have to help my friend. Tell me what happened."

"They paid me to show them the back door and to saddle her horse while they were inside. Then they carried out your friend. When they left, they said they would come back for you."

"Will you help me?"

The hostler hesitated. He seemed embarrassed by the story he had just told. "What do you want?"

"Saddle my horse and tell me which way they went."

The hostler nodded and slowly got to his feet. "I'll help you. They took your friend through the gate." He walked toward the horses.

"What?" Steve followed him. "Don't the guards close the gate at night?"

"Yes. They bribed the sentries to open it for them. I saw them in the light of the torches." The hostler went inside the stable.

Steve waited for him outside and looked toward the gate in the Great Wall. Torches burned over the gate, but no guards were posted down on the road now. He could see firelight flickering in the windows of the watchtower over the gate; obviously, that was where the night watch spent their hours on duty.

A moment later, the hostler led his horse out with a halter and tied it loosely to a pole.

"Can the sentries normally be bribed that way?"

"Yes, the Chinese guards can be. But not the Mongols, if you see any." The hostler went back inside the stable and came out with Steve's saddle.

"How much does it take?"

The hostler threw on the saddle and adjusted its position. "What you gave me would do it, but each man who comes down from the watchtower must have the same." He drew the girth up under the horse and cinched it.

"How many are there?"

"Only two men are on watch. Sometimes only one wants to come down. Maybe the other is asleep, or just doesn't want to bother." The old man slipped off the halter and put on the bridle. When he had fastened it, he handed the reins to Steve.

"I expect to be back tonight with my friend," said Steve. "We'll want you to take care of our horses again." He put his foot in the stirrup and swung up into the saddle.

The old man nodded.

Steve looked up into the sky. The moon was high and threw enough light to see the ground. Still, he had no idea what kind of terrain he was about to cross.

He nudged his mount forward and reached up to unhook the lantern that hung over the stable. "I'll bring this back if I can." Then, holding the lantern in one hand, he rode toward the gate in the Great Wall.

Marcia rode through the darkness more frightened than she had ever been. Her wrists had been lashed together, then tied to the front of her saddle. One of her kidnappers held the reins of her horse.

Her captors did not have a lantern. They kept to the road as it wound across open areas of steppe, away from the forest. Moonlight lit the way north.

During the first terrifying moments when her kidnappers had come into her room, she had been gagged almost immediately. As she tried to resist them, she had been able to switch on her lapel pin before her hands had been tied. Then her captors had carried her out of the room and down some back stairs in near silence.

The old hostler had been waiting with her horse. In the light of the small lantern at the stable, she had finally counted five kidnappers, one of whom had taken the reins of her mount and tied them to his own saddle. They had paused to dicker with the sentries at the gate in the Great Wall, but the sentries had ignored the gag tied over her mouth.

These sentries were not the same men Steve had spoken to earlier. Obviously, the watch had changed since then. These sentries were more interested in the bribe they received for opening the gate after dark than in interfering with other people's business.

No one spoke. Marcia rode at a walk through the moonlight, listening to the clopping of the horses' hooves. She supposed the lead rider had to go slowly because of the near-darkness. Certainly she would not complain; wherever they were taking her, she hoped the trip took a very long time.

The road curved as it skirted the edges of the forest, rising and dipping steeply at times. Ahead and to her left, Marcia could see lights clumped together in the distance; she decided they were torches or camp fires at the Mongol camp. She could not tell how far the camp was, but her captors clearly had no intention of going any closer.

Marcia had no idea if she could realistically expect any help. Hunter might still be too far to receive the sound of hoofbeats through her lapel pin. Even if he were receiving them right now, he could be too far back down the road to catch up before something horrible happened to her.

Steve, for all she knew, could still be enjoying his dinner with the Mongols. He certainly had to keep his lapel pin turned off while he remained in their company. Besides, when he did discover that she was missing, he would be alone without a robot to help rescue her.

The riders around her pulled up for a moment on the crest of small hill; the man holding Marcia's reins drew her mount to a stop with them. In the pale moonlight, she saw that the road forked, one branch angling to the left toward the Mongol camp. The other branch continued north.

"What are we going to do?" One man, merely a shadow to Marcia, turned in his saddle to look at the others. "Which way shall we go?"

"I say we are far enough," said another. "We must do what we are going to do."

Marcia felt herself go cold deep inside.

"I do not like it," said a third man in a high, whiny voice. "She will be found here, and the sentries at the wall will remember us."

"She deals with evil spirits," someone else reminded him. "We must kill her and return to the inn before evil spirits come to save her and kill us all."

"We have to kill her friend as well," said the first man. "We must finish with her in time to return for him and bring him back out here."

"At least we must take her away from the road," said the man with the whiny voice, "into the trees where her body will not be found until we are far away, if ever."

"Who will do it?" The first man asked. "One of you soldiers? You have the swords."

"I am a soldier, not a murderer," someone said stiffly. "Anyone of us can do the job."

"We are all in this together now," said another, "no matter who actually does it."

No one spoke for a long moment. Marcia could hardly believe she was listening to them discuss killing her. She could not believe she was going to die in this year, centuries before she had been born.

"Either all of us must kill her or none of us," said the first man.

Marcia understood their dilemma. They were not murderers by nature. However, they were highly superstitious and were driven by their fear of her.

"We cannot let her live now," said one of the others. "She will call evil spirits down on us."

"I have an idea," said the man with the whiny voice. "We can leave her out in the woods, tied, without her outer robes. The heat of the day and the cold of the night will do the work, or maybe wild animals."

"This is good," said the first man. "We shall be equally responsible."

Marcia could see the heads of all her captors nodding in the moonlight. None had the stomach for killing her outright. They wanted to take the easy way out.

"Yes, I agree," said another man. "Nature can do the job for us. And we can return for her friend."

"Fine," said the first man. "Now we must move away from the road and find a place to leave her."

Marcia tried to swallow, but her throat was too dry.

Steve rode north from the Great Wall at a trot. That speed was risky in the moonlight on a bad road, but it was his only chance to catch up to Marcia and her kidnappers. He hoped that they had been traveling at a walk ever since they had left. If not, he had no chance of catching up.

He held the lantern forward as he rode, to see the fresh tracks he was following. While those tracks were not much newer than the other tracks left by the day's travelers, they overlaid the earlier tracks with clear imprints on the dry, dusty road. He knew they might leave the road at any time, and he had to spot the location immediately if they did. Since Hunter, with his enhanced vision, had failed to notice where Wayne's group had left the road last night, Steve was acutely aware of how easy it would be to miss this.

Through the shadows in the moonlight, Steve kept his gaze on the road. He left his lapel pin turned on. It provided him with the sounds of hoofbeats of the riders ahead of him. Gradually, he heard those hoofbeats grow louder as he gained ground on the steep, rolling slopes.

When Steve heard voices coming from his lapel pin, he listened carefully. He heard Marcia's captors discuss their plans for her. From his own point of view, having Marcia tied up and abandoned was not bad at all. If he could avoid her kidnappers on their return trip, he could find her through the lapel pin and free her.

However, he did not like the uncertainty in their voices. He was afraid they might change their minds and kill her outright afer all. That meant he still had to rescue her if he could.

Steve wanted to form a plan, but he was not sure how to proceed. From the volume and clarity of the hoofbeats coming through his lapel pin, he knew that he was not too far behind them now. He guessed the distance at about thirty meters, a distance at which he could still not hear their hoofbeats clearly without the radio signal. Apparently they were behind some hill.

Steve paused to blow out the flame inside the lantern he carried. Otherwise, Marcia's captors would see the glow as he drew closer. They would not hear his hoofbeats for a while yet because the sound of their own would camouflage his.

Steve wished he could confer with Marcia. He wanted to reassure her that he was nearby and also plan her escape with her. Of course, her captors would hear his voice.

Then he realized that he could use that to his advantage. After all, they believed that he and Marcia dealt in evil spirits. Hearing his voice through her lapel pin now would not make any difference.

"Marcia, Steve here," he said in English. "I'm right behind you."

He heard a roar of startled shouts from the men in the background.

"Mmmmmm."

"Marcia, you okay? Is that you?"

"Mmm."

Steve realized, then, that she was gagged.

The men were still gasping, then shouting, in awe at the sound of a man's voice from nowhere.

Steve switched to Chinese. "Do not harm this woman," he intoned authoritatively. "She is under the protection of good spirits. Beware."

"Hunter here." The robot's voice was weak and nearly drowned out by static. "Since you are not afraid of being overheard, I can say I am much closer to you now than I have been all day. Marcia must be in trouble. I am riding as fast as I can, but my mount is very tired."

"Where are you, Hunter?" Steve asked. "We need help. I don't have any weapons or anything."

"I can see lights in what I believe is a watchtower in the Great Wall ahead, but I am not close to it yet. Right now, I am on the crest of a hill, looking across a considerable distance."

"We don't have time for you to catch up," said Steve. "Follow us if you can."

Up ahead in the moonlight, Steve saw the shadows of the group on horseback. His only advantage was their fear of evil spirits, so he decided to give them another scare if he could. Suddenly kicking his mount hard into a gallop, he screamed as loud as he could and rode straight toward them.

With panicked shouts, the riders in front of him all turned and fled. He could see Marcia's silhouette momentarily in the moonlight. Her mount suddenly took off away from the road, over a rolling hill.

Steve saw that her arms angled down to the pommel of the saddle and suddenly realized that her horse was out of control. He reined after her and kicked his mount hard. "Hang on!"

Marcia was helpless on her breakneck ride through the near-darkness. At any moment, her horse could stumble in the moonlight, throwing her out of the saddle and then dragging her by her wrists. If his own mount fell, he might never catch up to her.

"Turn your horse!" Steve shouted to Marcia. "Use your knees, elbows, lean against the side of his neck, anything! Try to slow down!"

Steve knew that she couldn't actually turn her mount completely. However, she might slow him down, even make him turn a little. Now, Steve could see that he was gaining ground on Marcia.

Her horse went over the crest of a rounded hill and down a steep slope. Marcia leaned to one side in the saddle, struggling to steer her horse to the right. Steve rode hard and gradually came up on her left. Her reins would be trailing loose from her horse's bridle.

Steve leaned forward over his mount's neck, still riding hard. He looped his reins over his left wrist and shifted the paper lantern to his left hand. With his right hand, he reached out and flailed in the dark for Marcia's reins. Suddenly his hand snagged the loose, unseen reins and he jerked them taut.

"Whoa!" Steve drew back, reining in his own mount and also Marcia's.

Back on the road, the other riders did not stop. They rode on into the darkness. In a moment, even their shadows were lost around the next bend.

Steve and Marcia finally came to a halt. He maneuvered his horse next to hers so he could reach her gag. She leaned toward him to make it easier.

"Got her, Hunter." Steve reached over and untied the cloth around Marcia's mouth. "You okay?"

"Yes," she said breathlessly, nodding. "But my hands are tied."

"I am glad," Hunter said, his voice still sounding distant through the static.

"We have to hurry," said Steve. "I'm afraid those guys will gather their wits and come back for us." He wished he still had the knife he had carried on their second mission in Jamaica during the seventeenth century. Instead of cutting Marcia loose, he had to untie her. Finally he pulled her bonds free, and she rubbed her sore wrists.

"Can you handle your reins?" Steve asked.

"Yes, I think so."

"Good. Let's go." Steve turned his mount and kicked it to a trot. Marcia kept pace.

"Hunter, we're heading back south at a trot. The guys who kidnapped Marcia are riding fast in the other direction, but I'm afraid they may change their minds."

"I understand," said Hunter. His voice came through slightly more distinctly than before. "I read you more clearly now. I have almost reached the small town by the gate in the Great Wall. I hope to join you soon."

"Good," said Steve, "just in case they come back. But you'll have to bribe your way through the gate. If we're lucky, the kidnappers won't stop running till they reach Siberia. We just can't take that chance."

As they rode, Steve glanced back over his shoulder. He saw no sign of the other men behind them, nor did he hear them. Maybe they truly were too frightened to stop fleeing anytime soon.

In the distance to his right, he could still see the lights of the Mongol camp in the distance. Some of the camp fires had burned down, but others remained as bright as ever. He supposed that Timur and the other sentries kept some fires burning all night.

Steve and Marcia rode side by side at an urgent trot. Every so often, he turned to look behind them again, but he still saw no one. At times, the moonlight outlined the crenellations atop the Great Wall and the watchtower over the gate ahead of them. Then the road would dip and take them out of sight of the Great Wall again.

They had ridden for some time when suddenly the dark silhouettes of men on horseback moved out from behind a small bluff. The riders crossed the road at a walk in front of Steve and Marcia. Then they calmly turned to face them and stopped to block the way.

Startled, Steve yanked back on the reins and started to turn. He saw more riders moving around them on each side. Behind them, several more blocked the road. Marcia, looking around frantically, gasped in surprise.

"Who are you?" A voice demanded in Mongol. "Where are you going at this hour?"

"Back to the Great Wall," Steve said politely in the same language.

Suddenly one of the other riders made a clicking sound and lit a torch. Steve winced in the sudden light, then saw that the Mongol raising the torch held a flint and steel in his other hand. By the flickering orange torchlight, Steve recognized Timur as the man who had spoken.

"Ah!" Timur grinned, seeing Steve's face clearly for the first time. "So, it is my friend from dinner!"

Steve smiled back Timur, relieved to see him in a friendly frame of mind. "Good evening."

"What are you doing out here in the middle of the night, my friend?" In the flickering torchlight, Timur glanced at Marcia, then back at Steve.

"Be careful," Marcia whispered in English. "Kidnapping probably gets the death penalty here. Almost every serious crime does."

Steve understood her point. They did not want to cause her kidnappers, or anyone else, to die. Already, the team had influenced local people to take many actions they would not have otherwise taken.

"We had a misunderstanding with some of our fellow travelers, but it is settled now. I apologize for the inconvenience to you and your men."

"We can find these people for you. Perhaps you want them punished."

"No! No, the problem has ended. I gave them a good scare myself." Steve glanced at the riders around them, hoping to change the subject. "You must have brought all the sentries out with you."

Timur chuckled, and so did many of his companions. "No, my friend. Most of the sentries remain on duty. I saw a mysterious light out here a short while ago and woke up a squad of riders to join me in finding it."

"It was just this." Steve lifted up the paper lantern. "I first saw it moving north. By the time we got out here, we heard you returning and took our positions to intercept you."

"You were very quiet," said Steve. He figured a compliment couldn't hurt. "I had no idea you were coming toward us or waiting here."

Timur simply nodded casually. "We shall escort you back through the gate." He turned his horse, and his men imitated his movement. The rough circle of men around Steve and Marcia began to ride south at a walk.

Steve exchanged a glance with Marcia, and they kept pace. He felt safe from Marcia's kidnappers, but he also knew that Timur was not giving them any options. Their host wanted them returned to where they belonged. In any case, they were now safe from Marcia's kidnappers, even if that group did turn around and come back.

"You're okay?" Steve asked Marcia quietly in English. He was not asking for information. Instead, he wanted to convey a message to Hunter, who undoubtedly had heard the entire conversation with Timur. He would still be listening, concerned about their condition.

"I'm fine," she said clearly.

"So am I." Steve grinned, sure that she understood what he was doing.

Tired after a long day of riding, Steve would not have minded moving faster. His mount was weary, however, and he decided that asking the Mongols for more speed might lead to a full gallop. He definitely had had enough breakneck riding for one night. So he said nothing and simply gazed up at the Great Wall in the moonlight as they returned to it.

Under the watchtower, Timur reined in. As his companion raised the torch high, the other riders also stopped. In the windows of the watchtower, sentries looked out, their silhouettes outlined against the light of their own fire inside the watchtower.

"Open the gate," Timur shouted in his accented Chinese. "Open for two lost travelers."

"The gate opens in the morning," a sentry called back. "Who is there?"

"You know me," Timur growled angrily. He rose up in his stirrups. "Open this gate *now!*"

The man with the torch held it so that the light fell clearly across Timur's face. The sentry who had spoken disappeared from sight. Several of the Mongols had already nocked arrows to their bowstrings.

Steve held himself motionless, hoping that no violence would begin. Next to him, Marcia gasped slightly. He saw now just how arrogant and quick to anger the Mongols could be toward the Chinese.

After several moments, the gate opened with a creak. A single Chinese sentry drew it open, staring at the Mongols fearfully. Timur rode forward, as did the man holding the torch, and stopped right in front of the open gateway.

"Our friends must return to their inn," Timur said with cold authority. "Tomorrow I may return through this gate to visit with them again. When I do, I will want to hear that all has gone well for them."

The sentry nodded quickly.

Still looking down at him, Timur waved Steve and Marcia forward.

Steve rode carefully, glancing at Marcia to make

sure she was coming with him. They passed without a word through the arched gate. On the other side, Steve turned.

"Thank you, Timur," he called in Mongol. "Good evening to you all."

"Farewell!" Timur waved once, then turned his mount and trotted away in the torchlight of his companion. The other Mongols rode after him, and they all vanished quickly into the darkness.

The sentry sighed loudly, letting his shoulders sag, and closed the gate again.

Steve reached into his pouch for a coin. Timur's warning to the sentry would probably carry a great deal of weight, but a modest token of generosity would not hurt, either. He tossed a coin to the sentry, who fumbled for it with a surprised look and then had to pick it up off the ground. The sentry gave him a nod of thanks.

As the sentry hurried back up inside the watchtower, Steve rode toward the inn. The stable was dark; the hostler had either gone to bed or was hiding. Steve hung up the paper lantern where he had found it.

"Wait a minute," said Marcia, following him reluctantly. "We can't go back to the same inn."

"Hunter, Steve and Marcia here," Steve said quietly. "Where are you?"

"Here," said Hunter aloud, stepping out from behind one corner of the inn. He held the reins to his tired mount and Jane's, as well. "I am relieved to see that you are both well. I continued to receive your transmission, so I knew you were coming back safely."

"But now what are we going to do?" Marcia asked. "I'm so tired."

"So are all the horses," said Steve. "They're probably ready to drop."

"The inn is unsafe," said Hunter. "The people who have now kidnapped three of us may still be able to return tonight."

"That's right," said Marcia.

"Yeah, that makes sense," said Steve. "So let's go back to my original idea—use the sphere to follow Wayne and Ishihara back to Khanbaliq."

"Can we?" Marcia asked hopefully.

"Why not?" Steve said. "We can get a good night's sleep."

"I like the sound of that," said Marcia, smiling weakly. "I'm really cold. And I hurt from all the riding. I'd love to skip the ride back."

"I do not like the sound of it," said Hunter firmly. "We must ride."

"Why?" Steve asked. "If we jump back, we won't have to worry any more about a bunch of guys who were last seen riding off north of the Great Wall in the dark. And Wayne won't have an advantage over us after all. Tomorrow morning, we'll be right back in the search for MC 5."

"We must return the horses to the city," said Hunter. "So we must ride them."

"That's a two-day advantage for Wayne and Ishihara," said Steve. "Not to mention that we don't know where to spend the night."

"I will protect you now from further harm," said Hunter. "We will remain together. We will not be surprised or overpowered again."

"But what if Wayne finds MC 5 during the next couple of days?" Steve demanded.

"We must return the horses," said Hunter. "They cannot fit in the sphere with us safely."

"You know we could be throwing away the entire mission," said Steve urgently.

"Riding back is not ideal," said Hunter. "Of course I realize this."

"Look, we all got suckered into coming up here," said Steve. "The Polos never came this way at all. Wayne and Ishihara have given themselves a free hand."

"We bought the horses," said Marcia. "Why can't we sell them here?"

"Or even give them away," said Steve.

"We would be leaving a potentially serious change behind that we can prevent," said Hunter.

"Hold it right there," said Steve. "How serious can the horses be?"

"We cannot know," said Hunter. "That fact is the crucial point."

"Well, then, as you like to say, what is the likelihood? I don't think it can be very great."

"I disagree," said Hunter. "Horses are very important in this time."

"I think I may regret this," said Steve, with a sigh. "But would you explain exactly what harm we can do by selling our horses here?"

"If we leave ours here, they may provide transportation or additional income to people in this town who would not otherwise have had them. Conversely, we may at the same time deprive people in Khanbaliq of those advantages. We must return them to where we found them."

"I was right," Steve muttered.

"About what?" Marcia asked.

"I do regret asking."

"Then you accept my argument?" Hunter asked.

"Maybe not," Steve said slowly. "It just doesn't make sense to me."

"It's only four horses," said Marcia thoughtfully. She rubbed her folded arms harder.

"Hunter, horses *are* important here—but they're also very common," said Steve. "They're everywhere."

"That's true," said Marcia, with sudden enthusiasm. "In a society that uses horses all the time, they actually have somewhat less value than in our society. In our own time, owning a horse is a luxury, either for the very wealthy or for people like Steve, who live in a rural area where it's affordable. But in neither case is it a necessity."

"That's right," said Steve.

"I agree that the relative value is different in this society than in ours," said Hunter. "However, within the context of this society, horses are expensive and important to the people who own them or need them."

"Well, yes," Marcia said reluctantly.

"You know we've proven that the ordinary changes we've caused don't matter," said Steve. "On previous missions, we bought weapons in Port Royal and abandoned them in Panama. We took fur cloaks and moved weapons in ancient Germany, too. In the Soviet Union, we caused guys in cars to drive around looking for us and use up gas. We've already talked about how consuming food and water and air hasn't changed anything important in our own time. The horses just aren't much bigger than the changes we've already made."

"Your list of our past changes is correct, but I judge these horses to be more important. Weapons and clothing were undoubtedly moved in large numbers even without us in Morgan's mission from Jamaica to Panama and in the Battle of Teutoburger Wald. The mechanical resources and fuel used in the Battle of Moscow also far outstripped the consumption we caused. In each of those cases, our influence was subsumed by the larger events. However, in this case, the effect of leaving our horses would stand alone."

"Debating with you is exhausting," said Steve. "I see the logic in all the particulars. But if I look at the whole picture, I'm just not convinced that moving four ordinary horses will matter in the long run."

"I have no idea how these horses will spend the remainder of their lives," said Hunter. "I do know that leaving them here might help someone here, or hinder someone in Khanbaliq, at some indeterminate point in the future."

"I can't believe we're arguing endlessly about this in the middle of the night on the edge of Mongolia," said Marcia. "Where are we going to *sleep*? And *when?*"

"Why can't we do what Wayne did?" Steve asked suddenly. "However he managed to do it."

"What, exactly?" Hunter asked.

"We've already figured out that Wayne has somehow rigged his belt unit to move him and Ishihara in time without returning to the institute."

"That is the case," said Hunter.

"Well, can't you adjust our unit the same way?" Steve asked. "If Wayne could do it, you must be able to. Then we can all return, even with the horses, because the sphere won't be involved at all."

"Yes, I assume I can figure it out," said Hunter. "However, I do not want to further develop time travel technology. If humans gain wide use of it, they will do irreparable harm to themselves."

"You mean that's the only reason you haven't done it already?" Marcia asked in amazement.

"Yes. The First Law imperative."

"I don't get it." Steve sighed loudly. "Hunter, the technology *already* exists; we agreed a long time ago Wayne knows how to do it."

"Even so, the more this knowledge is confined, the better off humans will be."

"Hunter, look," Steve said impatiently, "the faster we grab Wayne and MC 5, the better off humans will be. How about *that* line of argument?"

"It is also logical."

"Good," said Steve. "Hunter, the time travel technology is going to be a problem no matter what we do tonight. You acknowledge that? "

"Yes, of course."

"Then suppose you figure out how to make us competitive with Wayne now, and we worry about how to handle the secret of time travel after we've finished our missions?"

"This has some logic, too," said Hunter.

"Now that Wayne has a two-day head start on us, I'd say it's extremely logical."

"All right." Hunter said nothing more, remaining completely motionless.

"What's wrong?" Marcia asked, staring at Hunter's immobile form.

"I don't think anything is wrong," said Steve. He understood that if a robot paused long enough for humans to notice, it meant he had a substantial amount of data to process. "He's probably studying the design of the sphere and the belt unit. Then he has to figure out what changes to make."

"Yes," said Hunter. "I see how to do it now. However, I require several minutes, at least, to alter the belt unit. I suggest you dismount, as well. Moving the horses with you on them is potentially dangerous."

"That's true," said Steve. "We don't want them falling on us." He dismounted. Until now, he had remained mounted in case they were going to continue riding.

Marcia did so, as well, and hugged herself with both arms. "I'm really cold."

Hunter also dismounted and gave his reins to Steve.

"We've had two very long days," said Steve. He watched Hunter as the robot opened the belt unit.

The shape of Hunter's right index finger stretched and reformed itself so that the end became a very finely shaped tool. Then he worked with it on the intricate insides of the unit. In less than a minute, he closed the unit and returned his finger to its normal shape.

"You finished already?" Steve asked.

"Yes, but I must test it first on myself."

"Wait a minute," said Steve. "You mean you're going without us?"

"Not to Khanbaliq."

"Huh? Where are you going, then?"

"I will simply jump about ten meters and half a minute into the future. Please remain where you are." Hunter walked a short distance away from Steve and Marcia. "The range of field may have changed without my realizing it. I want to make sure you are not carried with me."

Steve watched as Hunter vanished. For a long moment in the waning moonlight, Steve and Marcia stood silently holding the reins of their horses. A slight breeze rustled the trees.

Then Hunter appeared ten meters away, stumbling to catch his balance.

"It worked," said Marcia, with obvious relief. "Are you okay, Hunter?"

"I am fine," said Hunter, as he walked toward them. "However, I will take the horses to Khanbaliq first. If they stumble or fall, I will have the best chance to avoid them. Then I will return for you."

"Okay." Steve held out his reins. "What time are we jumping to?"

"Just one minute forward. That way, you will have time to get plenty of sleep." Hunter took the reins of all four horses and led them away from Steve and Marcia.

"And *where* are we going?" Marcia asked. "I mean, will we land outside the city again? And have another long ride back to the inn?"

"No. I recall a small stand of trees at the city market, not far from the inn by horseback ride. At this hour, I expect no one to be on the street there."

"Good," said Marcia, yawning.

Hunter and the animals vanished.

Then, almost instantly, Hunter reappeared.

"That was quick." Steve grinned.

"Not to me," said Hunter, walking up to them. "All the horses stumbled but did not fall. No one saw us arrive. I took the time to see that no one was coming from any direction, and to tie them to a tree. We will return only a moment after I left, again unseen by others."

"Sounds great to me," said Steve. He yawned, too. "Now?"

"Now," said Hunter.

Jane slept most of that first day back in the village near Khanbaliq. After the exhausting night out on the road by the Great Wall, she slept soundly even in the room with Wayne and Ishihara. On waking, she found Wayne gone but Ishihara sitting on the floor by the door of the room.

As soon as she stirred, the robot looked at her.

"How long have I been asleep?" Jane asked, sitting up. She stretched. The air in the room was hot and stuffy now; she had been sweating in her sleep.

"Eight hours, seventeen minutes, and twelve seconds," said Ishihara.

"So, I guess it must be the middle of the afternoon by now, huh?"

"Yes."

"Tell me where Wayne is."

"He rose about an hour ago. I believe he was hungry. He is somewhere in the village."

"Look, I need a trip to the latrine and I'm hungry, too. You know these are First Law concerns, even if it's not an emergency yet. What can you do about them?"

"I will make sure you have all your necessities," said Ishihara. "I must escort you, however. I have been instructed not to let you leave."

"Well, at the moment, that will do. I also want some water to wash up a little."

"Come with me."

Jane followed Ishihara outside.

In the shade near the door, a number of elderly villagers glanced up at her curiously as they threshed rice in small, hand-held wicker strainers.

Ishihara paused. "Food, please, for her."

An old woman nodded and got up. She hurried inside the house. The others returned to their work.

"She will need a few minutes to prepare it."

"Yeah, okay."

Ishihara led her to the latrine and then to the village well, where he raised a bucket of cool water for her.

"You may wash in it safely," said Ishihara. "Do not drink it unless it has been boiled. Some water inside has already been boiled for Wayne."

"All right."

"I wish I had my change of clothes," Jane muttered. "And a hairbrush."

Ishihara said nothing.

When Jane had washed her face and hands, and smoothed out her hair with her fingers, she glanced around. Some small children were running and laughing together as they played; others had stopped to stare at her. She smiled at them, then looked out at the fields surrounding the village, where she saw older children and adults working.

"Where can I eat?" Jane asked.

"This way."

Ishihara led her back into the house where she had slept. This time, they went back into the kitchen area, where the old woman squatted on a stone hearth. She stirred something sizzling in a pot that hung over the fire on a hook.

Jane moved closer and saw strips of meat and chopped greens sizzling in hot oil. She could not identify the meat or the vegetable by looking at them, though. She decided that perhaps she would rather not know. The food smelled good enough.

"The villagers consider us all honored guests," Ishihara said quietly. "The food they prepare for us is better than what they normally eat."

"I suppose that's more meat than they usually eat." Jane nodded. "Are we harming the village? What if they need more food later, maybe during the winter?"

"I have considered this," said Ishihara. "We must not stay here for long."

The old woman picked up a wooden bowl and used a long-handled wooden ladle to dish out the food. Then she placed a pair of chopsticks across the top of the bowl and held it up for Jane.

"Thank you." Jane accepted it.

The old woman nodded soberly and turned away.

"It's hot in here," Jane said to Ishihara. "Can I eat outside?"

"Yes."

Ishihara led her back outside. "Is this cool enough?"

The elderly villagers were still threshing rice. After brief glances up at Ishihara and Jane, they looked away again quickly. They still had a great deal of unthreshed rice.

"I think we make them uncomfortable. Is there some shade somewhere else?"

"Yes. You can sit under some trees on the west side of the village."

Jane nodded and followed Ishihara again. Around the corner of the building, she saw Wayne sitting under one of the trees. An empty bowl similar to hers lay on the ground near him, with chopticks angling out of it.

Ishihara stopped suddenly and looked back toward the dirt path leading through the fields toward the front of the village. Jane looked in the same direction. A small figure was riding up the path on a donkey.

"It is Xiao Li," said Ishihara.

"Did you say it's Xiao Li?" Wayne got to his feet and looked, too. "Hunter and his team couldn't have come back with him, could they?"

"I thought Hunter would take care of him, but I hear only the donkey. He is alone."

"I hope so," said Wayne.

"I guess he must be okay," said Jane. "I'm relieved." She picked up the chopsticks and began eating where she stood. "Ishihara, shouldn't you check on him?"

"Yes."

By this time, the elderly villagers had also seen the boy. A couple of them left their threshing to meet him. Ishihara hurried after them.

Wayne remained next to Jane.

"Don't worry," she muttered between mouthfuls. "I still can't outrun Ishihara. Besides, I don't have anywhere to go now. And I'm hungry."

"You get enough sleep?"

"Yeah."

Wayne nodded.

Over on the path, Ishihara lifted Xiao Li down from his donkey. The boy smiled and tolerated the questions of the two villagers who come to greet him. One escorted him inside; the other took the reins of his donkey.

"Weren't they mad," Jane asked, "when you and Ishihara came back without him?"

"No. They asked about him, but they don't seem to want to challenge what we do." Wayne hesitated. "I think that would change if we actually hurt someone. But I thought Hunter would find him."

"Your judgment isn't that good," said Jane, seeing a chance to raise some doubt in his mind. "Neither is Ishihara's, obviously. This whole situation could get out of hand."

Ishihara returned to them. "The boy seems to be all right. He said that he slept by the side of the road last night and then rode all day to come home."

"You could have caused extreme harm to him," Jane said sternly. "Your sense of the First Law is very poor. So is your overall judgment of human behavior and your reliance on Hunter when you didn't know if Hunter had even caught up to him."

"Don't listen to her," Wayne ordered. "If Xiao Li is okay, then you have not violated the First Law. She just wants to sabotage your efficiency."

"You have no efficiency," Jane declared. "Think about it, Ishihara. Think about the danger this boy was in, traveling that open road by himself."

"I'll have him lock you up alone," Wayne warned her. "If you'd rather enjoy the fresh air, then *shut up!*"

Jane shut up. She had already used her strongest arguments. However, she knew that Ishihara might not respond to them. Since Xiao Li had demonstrably survived his ordeal, Wayne was right; neither Ishihara nor Hunter had technically violated the First Law.

"It's too late to go into Khanbaliq today," said Wayne curtly to Ishihara.

"What is our plan?" Ishihara asked, with unusual stiffness in his manner.

Jane knew, then, that her comments had at least forced Ishihara to feel some doubt about his actions toward Xiao Li.

"We still have a good head start on Hunter," said Wayne brusquely. "Maybe a long head start, if he stays up near the Great Wall looking for all of us. We'll spend this evening in the village and get another night's sleep here. Tomorrow morning, we'll look for MC 5."

Steve woke up the next morning in his room in the inn back in Khanbaliq. He had not managed a full night's sleep, but he had rested enough to get on with the search for MC 5. As before, Hunter waited outside as he and Marcia dressed and washed. Then for breakfast they returned to the same stall they had visited on their first morning in the city.

Steve and Marcia again bought bowls of steaming rice gruel and plates of meat and vegetables to drop into the rice. They sat down at one of the long wooden tables, away from other patrons. Steve ate hungrily.

Next to him, Hunter stood by the end of their bench and looked up and down the street over the heads of the people eating at the nearby tables. Steve glanced up from his bowl and, as before, saw people from many lands crowding the street. They reminded him that Marco Polo really was around here somewhere.

"See anything interesting?" Steve asked. He was just making conversation; he knew very well that Hunter would announce any sighting of significance.

"I recognize many of the people I saw at this hour

on our first morning. I conclude they are living a regular routine, but this is irrelevant to our immediate goals."

"Well, what about those goals?" Marcia asked, between mouthfuls. "I'd feel much more comfortable if we could rescue Jane."

"I feel responsible for her," said Hunter. "However, I know that Ishihara will not let her come to harm. In contrast, we are racing Wayne to locate and apprehend MC 5. That search remains more urgent."

"We don't have to repeat this whole line of argument again, do we?" Steve shook his head. "Wayne *wants* us to be distracted by Jane's kidnapping. That alone should tell us that searching for her is not in our best interest."

"I accept your logic," said Hunter. "If I develop the slightest reason to believe that she might be in danger, however, the First Law will alter my priorities."

"Okay, understood," said Steve. "And I just realized something else that's important here—Jane's presence will actually help us, since Ishihara is now forced by the First Law to protect two humans."

"That's true," said Marcia. "She'll either be with them both, or Wayne will have to leave her imprisoned somewhere. I wonder what Ishihara would do then."

"My own interpretation of the First Law would require me to remain with her," said Hunter. "I would judge Wayne more capable of taking care of himself than a human who was held against her will."

"Wouldn't you want to keep them together?" Steve asked. "So you could protect both humans? Come to think of it, wouldn't you insist?"

"That's right," said Marcia. "You behave that way to some degree with us."

"Ideally, we would remain together," said Hunter. "However, I cannot guarantee exactly what interpretation of the First Law Ishihara will make."

"I think that if we search for MC 5, we may very well come across all three of them," said Steve. "And if we just get MC 5 first, we can save Jane after that."

"We have already discussed the heart of this matter," said Hunter. "I agree that our search for MC 5 should lead us to Jane."

"Then what's our plan of action?" Steve asked.

"Our original plan, of finding Marco Polo, is still good," said Hunter. "We allowed ourselves to be fooled, and I share responsibility for how easily we were drawn out of Khanbaliq. Even so, our goal remains sound."

"Well, as far as I know, he's here at home somewhere," said Marcia.

"Wherever that is," said Steve. "But instead of just asking around, and letting Wayne and Ishihara sucker us again, we should think of a more reliable way of finding him."

"We could go to the imperial palace of Kublai Khan," said Marcia. "Someone there—probably lots of people—must know where he lives."

"Lots of people?" Steve asked.

"Servants, mostly. Couriers who take messages back and forth—that kind of thing."

Steve nodded. "Makes sense."

"I prefer not to risk that," said Hunter. "Any involvement on our part with the palace is more likely to alter the future significantly than our dealings with common citizens. I want to avoid the palace if we can accomplish our goals without going there."

"Okay, what do you suggest?" Steve leaned back from his empty bowl.

"Perhaps some of the other foreign dignitaries or traders will know the residence of Marco Polo," said Hunter. "We certainly have many of them to ask. Marcia, what do you think? Will they cooperate?"

"It's possible." Marcia shrugged. She, too, had finished her breakfast. "It's as good as asking people on the street at random. I would suggest that you do the asking, however, in your role as a fellow foreign trader."

"I understand," said Hunter. "All right. I will make this attempt."

"Let's stay right here," Steve said to Marcia. "After all, we belong to the conquered people. Maybe he'll do better without us."

"Good point," said Marcia, with a trace of surprise in her voice.

Steve grinned. "Well, I'm learning."

Steve and Marcia watched Hunter walk out to the street. As usual, he towered over everyone around him. Hunter let the Chinese pass him. Steve saw him stop two men with dark curly beards and speak to them briefly.

"Where are they from?" Steve asked.

"Persia, I would say by their clothes."

Steve nodded, still watching Hunter.

The two men shook their heads and continued on their way down the street.

Hunter glanced around and approached a man in a long, colorfully embroidered robe. This man listened but did not stop walking. He merely shook his head and hurried past.

"How about that guy?" Steve asked.

"Maybe a Turk. I'm not sure."

"Hey, what about these two?" Steve nodded toward

two other men whom Hunter had stopped.

Both men were tall, with black hair and long, angular faces with carefully trimmed black beards. They wore white turbans and long, flowing robes. As one stood by impatiently, the other nodded and pointed with one arm.

"Arabs," Marcia said firmly.

"I guess they know something," said Steve.

After a moment, Hunter nodded and the two Arabs walked on their way.

"Come on." Steve got up and led Marcia over to Hunter. "Well? Did they know where to find him?"

"I have directions to the residence of Marco Polo. The man who pointed is a trader. In the course of his business, he has met Marco Polo and was once a guest briefly at his home. He does not know if Marco Polo is present today."

"We obviously should have done this the first time," said Steve.

"I had no idea it would be this easy," said Marcia. "This is embarrassing."

"If we had begun this way, Wayne might have also altered his plan to send us up to the Great Wall," said Hunter. "We did not make a simple mistake before; we were deliberately misled. However, the house of Marco Polo is nearby."

"Lead on," said Steve.

Hunter took them at a brisk walk down the crowded street toward the center of the city. The imperial palace rose above the other buildings in this area. Hunter saw that under the hot and unrelenting morning sun, Steve and Marcia were sweating heavily. He slowed down.

After several blocks, Hunter turned right along a smaller street. Here, tall trees lined the street, shading it from the sun. High walls of painted brick hid the houses from view except for their roofs, visible through treetops within each compound. The roofs were made of glazed tile that shone in the sunlight.

"This is it," Hunter said. He stopped at double doors set into a round archway in the wall. This wall was white; the doors were red. A small brass bell hung on the hook to one side of the doors.

"The home of Marco Polo," Marcia said quietly, looking up at the roof beyond the treetops. "Wow."

Steve smiled. Ever since Hunter had been kidnapped, Marcia's manner had been looser—more spontaneous and less stuffy. He realized that he had actually come to like her.

Hunter rang the little bell.

"We have to remember which languages to use," Marcia reminded them.

"Correct," said Hunter. "You two should not reveal that you can understand Italian, if he uses it. I will use it with him to make what I expect will be a positive impression. We can all speak Mongol with him."

"Won't he wonder how you learned it?" Steve asked. "I mean, supposedly, Marcia and I live in this empire, but you're from somewhere else."

"I will explain that I learned Mongol on my journey here."

The sound of a small door opening and closing reached them from beyond the wall. Steve heard footsteps on stone coming toward them.

"The servants could be Chinese, right?" Steve asked. "But then, how could he communicate with them?"

"Maybe they aren't," said Marcia.

"I will try Mongol with the first servant," said Hunter. "They must be bilingual if not multilingual. The question will be which languages they speak."

The red door opened. A tall, slender man with graying hair bowed perfunctorily and studied Hunter carefully, appraising his robes; he gave Steve and Marcia only a quick glance. However, he said nothing, waiting for Hunter to speak first.

"He's Chinese, isn't he?" Steve muttered.

Marcia nodded.

"I am Hunter, a trader from Europe," Hunter said in Mongol. "I arrived recently and would like to speak with the Venetian Marco Polo. Is he here?"

The servant looked at Steve and spoke in Chinese. "You can translate for your friend? What does he want?"

"I speak Chinese," said Hunter, in that language. He repeated his request to see Marco Polo.

"Please wait. I will return shortly." With a deeper bow this time, the servant closed the door again and hurried back to the house at a brisk walk.

"Well, he must be here," said Steve. "Otherwise, the servant could have told us he wasn't."

"Now the big question is whether he'll see us," said Marcia.

A moment later, the door of the house opened and closed again. The servant's footsteps tapped quickly on the stones as he hurried back. This time he drew both doors open, bowing deeply as he moved out of their way.

"Welcome, welcome. Please come in."

Hunter entered first. Steve waited for Marcia to go next, but she shook her head tightly. He followed Hunter and Marcia came in behind him. The servant closed the doors behind her.

The grounds were covered by a small, grassy lawn shaded by the trees they had seen over the wall. A leafy hedge lined the inside of the wall. A walk of precisely cut stones led to the front door.

The house itself had been constructed of wood, now painted white. The front door stood in the center, with precisely matched windows on each side; the entire building, down to every detail, was bilaterally symmetrical. Long, white curtains fluttered in the open windows.

The servant hurried from behind Marcia to beat Hunter to the front door. He flung it open and stepped aside, bowing again as his guests entered. Another servant, a young woman with long braids, held the door inside, also bowing.

The servants led them through a foyer into a large sitting room. Large tables of Chinese rosewood, small ones of black lacquer, and rosewood chairs lined the room. The chairs were padded with embroidered silk cushions; porcelain vases on the tables held green plants or flowers. Chinese landscape scrolls hung on the walls.

A European man of average height entered. He had curly brown hair and a neatly trimmed matching beard, and he wore a plain blue Chinese robe. Steve judged him to be in his late thirties.

"Welcome," he said in formally in Italian. "I am Marco Polo. Do you understand Italian?"

"Yes," Hunter responded in that language. "I am Hunter, a trader. My companions are close friends."

"Welcome," Polo said to Steve and Marcia in Chinese, with a slight bow.

"Thank you," said Steve, bowing. In the rear of the house, he could hear other footsteps and muffled conversation. Obviously, Polo employed many servants.

Next to him, Marcia also bowed but said nothing.

Switching back to Italian, Polo added, "I am not fluent in Chinese, but I have picked up a few words."

"You have done very well here," said Hunter.

"By your accent, you are not Italian," Polo said to Hunter. "Where are you from?"

"Switzerland."

"Switzerland! I have heard it is beautiful there. My travels never took me that direction."

Steve glanced quickly at Marcia. He did not recall Hunter discussing this detail of his role. She did not react, so Steve decided that Hunter knew what he was doing.

"However, I have traveled a great deal," said Hunter. "I have not been home for many years."

"Have you been to Venice? Can you bring me news of my home city?"

"I can tell you a little."

For the first time, Polo smiled broadly. "Excellent! Please sit down."

Steve waited for Hunter to move first. Hunter accepted a large rosewood chair. A small black lacquered table inlaid with abalone shell separated it from a matching chair that Polo took. Steve and Marcia then sat down on a small couchlike seat with a straight, uncomfortable back.

Polo turned to the servants, who were standing attentively to one side. "*Cha, dian xin.*"

The servants bowed and hurried away.

"He knows more Chinese words than you thought," Steve whispered. Polo had ordered tea and the brunch more commonly known in Cantonese as dim sum at home in their own time.

"So tell me about Venice," Polo said in Italian. "Is it still the premiere city in Italy?"

"It is proud and splendid," said Hunter, "the finest city in all of Europe."

"And Venetian galleys still sweep the Mediterranean of pirates?"

"Yes."

"I'm glad. I left when I was still young. My father and uncle are jewelers. They live in this neighborhood, too."

"How did your family first come here?"

"My father and my uncle had a house in Soldaia, on the Black Sea."

"That city has an entire colony of Italian merchants, doesn't it?"

"Yes! You've been there, I take it?"

"No," Hunter said. "I have heard of it."

"Oh. Well, it is a fine city, though not the equal of Venice—and certainly not the city that Khanbaliq is."

Steve relaxed, leaning back in his seat as Hunter and Polo discussed more events in Venice. He sneaked glances at Marcia, who did not react outwardly in any way. Steve realized that Hunter was using the information he had accessed from the Mojave Center library to convince Polo that he knew Venice.

Polo paused in the conversation as the servants hurried into the room with a big brass tray holding a porcelain teapot and four cups. Steve saw that Hunter followed Polo's lead and did not speak. The servants poured tea for everyone and handed them the small cups.

"Is the tea to your liking?" Polo asked. "The food will take a little longer, I fear."

"It is excellent tea," said Hunter.

Polo glanced at Steve and Marcia and spoke in Chinese. "Good?"

"Very good," said Steve.

Marcia nodded, smiling.

"Well, where was I?" Polo said, speaking Italian again. "My father and uncle journeyed from Soldaia to the land of the Golden Horde when I was a child."

"Much of modern Russia," Marcia whispered almost inaudibly to Steve.

"From that land, they came here to see Kublai Khan," Polo continued.

Hunter nodded, sipping his tea.

"When the khan heard of our religion, he asked them

to return home and have the pope send a hundred men learned in Christianity back with them, along with oil from the sacred lamp at the sepulchre in Jerusalem."

"Really?" Hunter asked politely. "Where were you during this time?"

"I was still in my youth. However, when my father and uncle returned, they invited me to travel back to China with them."

"I see."

"We took a couple of friars—the pope would not send a hundred—and some oil and started our journey." Polo smiled and shook his head. "The friars turned back out of fear, and we could not stop them. But we brought the oil, and we have been in the khan's empire ever since."

Steve took a deep breath and fought his impatience. This was mildly interesting, but accomplished nothing he could see. As Polo and Hunter continued to talk, he whispered to Marcia in Chinese.

"Why doesn't Hunter get to the point?" He spoke into her ear, still watching Polo and Hunter.

"This kind of slow exchange to get acquainted is part of business in this era," she whispered back. "In fact, as a social mannerism, it lasts largely up to the middle of the twentieth century."

"What's going on?"

"Business is very personal in this time. Certainly Polo knows Hunter came to ask for a favor, and he wants to get a sense of who the stranger is before he asks what Hunter wants. And Hunter seems to know this."

"Why doesn't Polo ask first what Hunter wants, and then decide if he wants to help?"

"That's considered rude."

"Oh."

"We'll just have to wait."

"If Polo continues to do most of the talking, though, I don't see what he can learn about Hunter." Steve straightened again and listened to Hunter and Polo.

"I have told my friends here a great deal about Europe and the lands between here and there," said Hunter, nodding toward Steve and Marcia.

"Kublai Khan is the greatest man of our time," said Polo. "Possibly of any time."

"Don't buy it," Marcia whispered to Steve in Chinese. "Polo never saw the large picture."

Steve remembered that when Marcia had first briefed the team, she had told them how the money had been devalued several times because the economy was poor. He also recalled that most serious crimes received the death penalty. This empire appeared prosperous, but economic mismanagement and rule by fear underlay life here.

The servants entered again, this time carrying two brass trays with dishes of steaming dumplings and noodles. They set the trays down on a large table and placed individual servings on small plates with chopsticks. Then they brought the servings to everyone.

Hunter and Polo resumed their conversation in Italian.

"Smells familiar," Steve whispered to Marcia. "It even looks the same as in our time."

"Much of the dim sum has been unchanged for centuries," said Marcia.

"Wait a minute. How do you know?" Steve grinned. "Food doesn't keep that long."

"Old recipes are still on record," said Marcia. She paused to blow on a hot dish. "Some dishes appear in paintings, relief sculpture, and book illustrations."

"Well, here's the real proof." Steve paused to eat.

"I'm fascinated just by meeting Marco Polo," said Marcia softly. "I just . . ."

"What?"

"I wish I could tell him about his book."

Steve glanced over at Polo and Hunter. Polo was listening to Hunter's story of their travels. Maybe they were making progress.

"What do you mean?" Steve whispered. "What do you want to tell him?"

"I wish I could tell him that after he returns to Italy, when the Genoese capture him in a war, not to worry. And that he'll tell stories of his travels in prison to a writer who sets it all down."

"He does it in prison?"

"Yes, as a prisoner of war. And I would warn him that much of what he says won't be believed in his own time, or for many years afterward, but that it will finally become a timeless classic."

"But you can't. It might influence him in the wrong way, somehow. As Hunter would say, then everyone who ever read his book might be a little different, too. The changes could really add up."

"I know."

Jane walked through the streets of Khanbaliq between Wayne and Ishihara. Wayne had wanted to leave her behind in the village, but Ishihara, under the imperative of the First Law, had refused to leave her with the villagers. Now Wayne and Ishihara were searching again for MC 5.

Many of the villagers had accompanied them to Khanbaliq this morning. Some tended their market stall, but others had taken time away from the fields to visit the city with the good spirits who had come to their village. Wayne had sent the others to fan out around Khanbaliq in search of MC 5, but Xiao Li had remained with them.

Jane had been thinking about how to escape Ishihara. Here, where some of the blocks were relatively crowded, she could probably dart away suddenly and have some chance of losing herself in the crowd. Since he could not risk harming her, the idea of trying to escape had become more attractive now that they were back in Khanbaliq in daylight instead of out in the forest at night.

However, she also saw several problems with this plan. For one, she had nowhere to go. She figured that Hunter and the rest of the team were either looking for her back on the road to the Great Wall, or else they were riding back to Khanbaliq.

Even if Hunter had decided to return to the sphere and come right back to Khanbaliq, she had no idea where in the city the team was now. The only meeting place they had used was the inn where they had spent the first night, but the team would not be waiting there at this time of day. Presumably, they would be out looking for her and MC 5.

Another problem was that she was so obviously a foreign visitor. She expected that if she ran, Wayne would order Ishihara to shout to all the people on the street in Chinese that she had to be captured. Since Wayne was also of European descent, she supposed that onlookers would assume they were together. For Wayne's purposes, any excuse to stop her would do, perhaps that she was crazed or drunk or even a thief. She could not outrun everybody.

Further, if her captors did not enlist the help of other people, the last problem was that Ishihara would inexorably follow her. She would gradually tire, while the sun replenished his solar converters with energy. Sooner or later, unless she had a safe haven very close, he would catch her again.

Finally, after she had attempted to run away, Ishihara would probably hold her arm continuously in the future. That meant she realistically had only one chance. In order to have a reasonable likelihood of success, she would have to wait until a particularly good opportunity developed. The best chance would come if she saw Hunter and the team somewhere on the street.

When Polo had seen that all his guests were well fed, he invited them into his study. Steve, holding his teacup, followed Polo and Hunter with Marcia at his side. The male servant waited outside the room, ready to be summoned.

Long wooden tables with intricately carved sides and legs lined the study. All were cluttered with a variety of objects. Steve saw scrolls of paper, Chinese ink sticks and brushes, and brass and porcelain bottles.

"The empire of Kublai Khan is full of wonders," said Polo. "Hunter, look at this." He lifted a long, narrow piece of blank paper and gently placed it over Hunter's open palms. "I suppose you think it's a kind of parchment."

Steve clenched his teeth together, fighting laughter. Marcia jabbed him in the ribs with her elbow. He took a deep breath and hid his smile behind his teacup.

Hunter looked at the paper closely, obviously pretending never to have seen it before. He brushed his fingertips across the surface. Then, as though it was tremendously valuable, he held it out for Polo to take back.

"How is it made?" Hunter asked. "It is clearly not parchment."

"No." Polo laid the sheet back down on the table. "Paper is made from pulping certain kinds of plants. The pulp is then suspended in a vat of water. When the mix is just right, a screen is placed in it and pressed. The pressing removes the water and makes it into these sheets. They are excellent for writing and painting."

"I have seen the Chinese write with their brushes," said Hunter. "Instead of using quill pens."

"In their language, the brush is very beautiful," said Polo. "Personally, I find it difficult to write the alphabet with it. I have tried many of these things you see on the tables around us, just to get the feel of them."

Hunter nodded.

Marcia jabbed Steve in the ribs again.

He looked at her in surprise. "What?" he whispered, mystified.

"The paper and brush."

"What about them? *I* can't write that way."

"Well, I can. I practiced a little as part of my historical studies. But you have to say something."

"Oh." Steve raised his voice and spoke in Chinese. "Hunter, she can demonstrate the brush for you and Marco."

"Eh?" Polo waited politely for Hunter to translate.

"May she show us?" Hunter asked in Italian. "I would like to see how the paper accepts the ink."

"Of course." Polo gestured for Marcia to come forward.

Steve sighed quietly. All this polite posturing made him very impatient. Somewhere in the city, Wayne and

Ishihara were dragging Jane around with them and might be on the verge of finding MC 5.

Marcia dipped the end of a slender, black ink stick in a pan of water and began grinding it in a shallow stone bowl designed for the purpose. She added more water from the pan and ground the stick again. After only a moment, she selected a narrow brush from a bamboo cylinder and dipped it in the liquid. The brush tip came out black.

"Watch closely," Polo said to Hunter.

Marcia slowly wrote a straight, horizontal line. Below it, she wrote two, the bottom one longer than the other. Then she wrote a character with three horizontal lines.

"Even I recognize those," Polo said with a smile. "The numbers one, two, and three."

Steve saw that the character for "four" was more complex; it was a rectangle with two squiggles inside.

Marcia wrote ten characters in all. Then she dipped the brush in the water pan, rinsed it, and laid it carefully across the ink bowl. With a slight bow, she stepped back out of the way.

"The characters have great beauty," said Polo. "I believe she has simply written from one to ten."

Hunter nodded, leaning over the paper. "This paper accepts the ink very well. It must be much cheaper than parchment. Is it widely used?"

"Yes." Polo picked up a large porcelain bowl of water. A flat, narrow piece of metal with a point on one end floated on top of it. "Hold this in your hand."

Hunter took it.

"Now turn the bowl so that the arrow points a different direction."

Hunter did so.

"Watch."

Steve saw that the arrow, bobbing slightly, slowly turned to point north. He suppressed a smile. At first, he hadn't recognized it as a compass.

"What is the significance of this needle?" Hunter asked politely.

Steve knew very well Hunter was still acting out his role. Beside him, Marcia turned away to hide her own smile of amusement. Not laughing at Polo had become a major challenge for both of them.

"It always points north," said Polo. "As travelers who have crossed uncountable miles, you and I know how helpful it could be."

"Yes, I see." Hunter gently laid down the bowl.

"You told my servant that you arrived recently in Khanbaliq. These wonders are all new to you?"

"They exist only here, do they not?" Hunter looked around at the other items on the long tables. "No one in Europe has ever seen them."

"That is true," said Marco. "I hope to bring some of them back to Venice someday."

Hunter nodded noncommittally.

"How can I help you?" Polo asked. "Do you need introductions here in the city, perhaps for your business?"

"I seek another foreigner, who goes by the nickname MC 5. He is a European, short and slight in stature."

"What is his trade?"

Steve tensed, wondering what Hunter would say.

"We believe he is seeking a post with the government," said Hunter.

"Ah, a civil servant." Polo nodded. "Has he been in Khanbaliq long?"

"No," said Hunter. "A few days at most, but maybe even less."

"I see." Polo turned to his servant in the doorway and spoke in heavily accented Chinese. "See to it."

The servant bowed quickly and hurried away.

Polo picked up a large porcelain bottle and pulled out the cork stopper. "Of all the wonders in the khan's empire, this is the most spectacular." He poured some gray powder out of the bottle into a small stone dish.

Steve looked at Marcia, puzzled. "What did he mean when he told his servant to 'see to it,' about MC 5?" he whispered in Chinese.

"I think the head servant will probably order some of the others to go to the palace or ask their other contacts in the city," said Marcia.

The servant returned to the doorway. Polo pointed to the gray powder. The servant bowed, then left again.

Steve looked back at the substance in the dish. He was fairly sure it was gunpowder. When he glanced at Marcia, she shrugged almost imperceptibly.

Without speaking, Polo cut a short piece of string from a roll with a small knife. Then he rolled the string in the powder until it was gray. He pulled it out so that the string overhung the edge of the dish and then laid it down.

The servant returned with a burning candle in a brass holder. Polo took it from him. Then the servant returned to the doorway again.

"Watch carefully," said Polo.

Steve suppressed a smile and caught Marcia's eye. She, too, was fighting a laugh. Hunter, of course, looked as though he had no idea what was about to happen.

Polo lit the fuse. It fizzed, sparked, and crackled. The line of fire quickly moved into the dish, where the remaining powder burned as well. Marco set the candle down on the table and stepped back.

When the gunpowder had burned down, the servant came back into the room. He leaned over the table to open a window, then picked up a small fan. As Polo moved out of his way, he waved the smoke toward the open window.

"Your companions are amused because this is old and familiar to them," said Polo pleasantly. "But you must understand the power of this substance. When tightly packed in a container, it explodes with great force. When a hole for the release of the fire and smoke is provided, it can make the container fly up into the air." He looked at Hunter for his reaction.

"Indeed?" Hunter said cautiously.

"A container of this type can send fire many times farther than a burning arrow," Marco said grimly.

Hunter simply nodded.

Steve realized that Hunter did not want to enter a discussion about the potential of gunpowder. Anything he said could alter what Polo would later write in his memoirs. None of them dared react very much.

"I, too, was shocked by the idea," said Polo. "But you will get used to seeing many wonders here in this empire if you stay long. Come. Let us return to the sitting room."

Steve took his seat again in the front room and accepted more tea, poured by the young woman servant. Marcia sat next to him, as before. Hunter and Polo continued their talk about the wonders of Kublai Khan's empire.

Steve could still hear other servants in the back of the house. Meanwhile, the two servants who had already attended them carried away the leftover food. Moments later, they brought out more of the same—fresh and steaming.

"I'm full," Steve muttered in Chinese to Marcia.

"It's part of the courtesy here," said Marcia. "Food will be available as long as we keep eating it. When we left the room, it wasn't because we had finished but because our host wanted to show us around."

Finally, as Polo and Hunter discussed politics within the far-flung empire of the khan, the head servant came in with a younger Chinese man, who was sweaty and breathless. Polo looked up.

"Yes?"

"Xiao Sung has information for your guests, sir," he said in Mongol.

"All right. Xiao Sung, go ahead."

Xiao Sung took a deep breath and spoke in Chinese. "I may have located him in the khan's palace."

"Excellent!" Polo turned to Hunter. "Even I understand that much Chinese."

"How do you know?" Hunter asked.

"I spoke to a courier whom Master Polo knows. He works at the palace. On the palace grounds, he saw a new courier, hired only a few days ago, who fits the description."

"Has he spoken to this new courier?" Hunter asked. "MC 5 has a language problem here. To my knowledge, he does not speak any of the prevailing languages, though he can learn languages quickly."

"No, our acquaintance did not speak to this man," said Xiao Sung. "But many languages are used in Khanbaliq. If he is the man you seek, he may have been able to communicate with at least some foreign guests."

"Couriers who cannot gossip are in great demand," said Polo. "They betray fewer confidences. All they must do is deliver written messages or packages faithfully to the right location or individual."

"A stranger can just arrive in the city and work in the palace of the khan?" Hunter asked. "Without references or introductions?"

"Foreign arrivals have a better chance of working in the palace than the local Chinese," said Polo. "The Chinese are considered a danger within the palace walls, since they are the conquered people here. And because the number of foreign people who will come here cannot be predicted, they are often welcomed quickly into certain jobs."

"I see," said Hunter.

"MC 5 could get the post of courier, but he will be closely watched during his first months on the job to see that he is reliable. Within the palace grounds, his movements will be severely restricted. He will be assigned to accompany a trusted courier during this time, to learn his way around and to earn the trust of his superiors."

"Then we must learn if this new courier really is MC 5," said Hunter.

Polo frowned thoughtfully. "To your knowledge, could he be a danger of any kind to the khan?"

"No," said Hunter. "In fact, if given the opportunity, he would risk his own well-being to save the khan's life. But he might wish to gain the ear of the khan someday and offer some opinions."

Polo laughed. "Nearly everyone in the empire would love to have the khan's ear for one reason or another." He glanced at Xiao Sung. "Is that all?"

"He has more, master," the head servant said politely.

"Oh. Please go on."

"I must also inform you that a search for an evil spirit of the description of this man called MC 5 is already underway in the streets."

"Eh?" Polo glanced at Hunter. "My Chinese is poor, but did he say that a search on the streets has already begun for this man?"

"Yes," said Hunter. "A business rival of mine also hopes to make contact with him."

"Ah! I see."

"Supposedly, a couple of good spirits have come down from the sky to capture MC 5," said Xiao Sung.

"What do they look like?" Steve asked suddenly in Chinese.

"Like foreigners," said Xiao Sung. "They resemble Master Polo and your friend, in a general way."

Steve grinned and glanced at Hunter. "Yeah, that's our business rival, playing games. Have they offered a reward for finding MC 5?"

"No, sir," said Xiao Sung. "No reward is offered, but the more superstitious people in this part of the city are looking for him."

"Do *you* believe in evil spirits?" Steve grinned at Xiao Sung. "Does everybody?"

"Of course, sir," said Xiao Sung, frowning in puzzlement. "But I do not confuse every foreign guest with visitors from the spirit world."

"Good," said Steve.

"Would it be possible to receive a letter of introduction from you?" Hunter asked. "I must go to the palace and see this new courier for myself."

"I will do more than that," said Polo. "Several days ago, I reported to the khan on my most recent trip out to the provinces. Now I am taking a week or so to relax, which leaves me free today. I, too, am curious about this mysterious stranger, so I will take you to the palace myself."

"I am imposing on you," said Hunter.

"Nonsense. I will enjoy the walk."

"Then I am in your debt."

Polo glanced up at this servants. "You will accompany us," he said in Mongol.

The servants left the house first, followed by Polo and Hunter. Steve and Marcia walked behind them. The young woman servant followed, first closing the front door behind them and then the gate in the wall.

"Hunter is going to be worried even more about altering Polo's actions," Steve said quietly.

"That's true. Well, Polo was always welcome at court, so this isn't likely to be too significant." Marcia took a deep breath. "I can hardly believe it. I'm about to see the palace of Kublai Khan."

Ishihara waited as Wayne and Jane took a break under a large tree on the edge of a city street.

"Look," said Xiao Li. "One of my cousins is running through the crowd toward us." He pointed.

Ishihara looked. A young man from the village dodged around a peddler's cart and stopped, breathing hard. "Your friend has been seen."

"Where?" Ishihara asked.

Beside him, both Wayne and Jane tensed.

"A man saw him deliver a message from the palace of the Emperor to the home of a general, then return again."

"What did he say?" Wayne asked in English, impatiently. "Does he know something?"

"He went to work in the palace," said Ishihara in English. "The seat of power."

"You will come?" The man looked back and forth between Wayne and Ishihara. "If an evil spirit is working in the court, he may cause harm for everyone."

"He is *not* an evil spirit, remember," said Ishihara. "He is merely a misguided spirit who belongs with us. We will take him away from the court if someone will take us inside the palace grounds."

"My mother's cousin is a minor attendant to one of the princes in the court. He will come to the gate if I ask the guard to call him."

"Can he let us in?" Ishihara asked.

"I believe so," the other man said slowly. "I have never tried before."

"Will we be stopped inside?" Ishihara asked. "We cannot disturb the palace routine."

"That's right," said Jane. "We can't afford to cause any trouble, remember?"

"My mother's cousin has often said that the palace grounds are like a separate city within Khanbaliq. Thousands of bureaucrats, servants, and other workers do their daily duties inside the walls."

"This is acceptable," said Ishihara. "A few more people can get lost in the crowd during the day. Will you take us to the palace?"

"I am at your service."

"Good."

"Are we going?" Wayne asked in English again. "Can we get to MC 5?"

"Yes," said Ishihara.

Steve stared at the towering walls around the palace grounds as he drew near behind Polo and Hunter. The grounds covered the equivalent of many city blocks, though Steve could not judge how many from this perspective. The walls rose up at least as high as the Great Wall. Sentries stood guard outside the closed gates. When they recognized Marco Polo, however, they bowed and opened the gates without comment.

Within the walls, the palace grounds were also laid out in the manner of a city. Broad walkways and large buildings lined up on a right-angle grid. Trees shaded the walks and the buildings. Marcia took his arm and pointed.

"See that long building with the statues by the entrance and the wooden threshold? By the architecture and the statues, I think that's a temple of some kind."

Steve nodded. "How about the other buildings?"

"I can't be sure of most of them. These buildings did not last into our time. Too many are made of wood, and they were replaced one by one as the centuries went by." Marcia looked to each side, then into the distance. She pointed to a huge edifice topped by a roof of vermilion, yellow, green, blue, and red, shimmering in the sunlight. "The largest building is the palace itself. In Marco Polo's book, he says the palace is the greatest that ever existed. He wrote that the largest hall can hold six thousand people at dinner. The khan's quarters are there, and those of his four wives."

"Yeah?"

"And the other buildings must house various bureaucratic offices."

"I wonder if there's any chance we could see Kublai Khan himself."

In front of them, Polo and his entourage came to a halt. Polo spoke briefly to a young man in a long, black robe who bowed deeply and hurried away. Then Polo turned to Hunter with an amused smile.

"I have been fortunate to enjoy the khan's favor ever since we arrived here. Many of the attendants know me; that man recently passed the examinations necessary to enter government service. He will speak to the chief of the palace couriers, and bring MC 5 to us."

"Thank you," said Hunter.

"It's going to be that easy?" Steve muttered to Marcia. "Hard to believe."

"Dr. Nystrom sent us on a long detour to the Great Wall. I just hope Jane's all right."

"Of course she is, in Ishihara's company." Steve

shrugged. "Well, MC 5 isn't here yet. So our search hasn't exactly succeeded."

"Come," Polo said to Hunter. "Now we will sit down and wait." He gestured forward, and his servants led the small entourage again.

This time the group walked to a shaded garden with a lawn and a hedge of flowering shrubs. Carved stone chairs surrounded a round table of matching stone. The servants stood under a nearby tree, waiting patiently as the others sat around the table.

"If we must wait long, I shall send for tea," said Polo. He leaned back in his chair. "What do you think of the palace grounds so far?"

"It is very impressive," said Hunter. "Efficiently laid out and well tended."

Polo laughed lightly. "You have an odd way of speaking, my friend. It is beautiful here, is it not?"

"Yes," said Hunter.

"You know, in the spring—" Suddenly Polo stopped talking, his eyes on a small group of people approaching them. "The khan! Do as I do." Polo leaped to his feet. He bowed very low from the waist and held the position. "Speak only if he bids you. Do not address him directly. Say, 'the khan,' or the 'great khan,' as though you are talking about someone not here."

Hunter rose and imitated Polo precisely.

Steve, startled, also got up and bowed; next to him, Marcia did the same. Around them, the servants had reacted more quickly and also stood motionless in their position. Steve sneaked a glance at the khan.

The man who stopped in front of Polo, frowning, had sharp, dark eyes and a ruddy complexion. His long, narrow mustache and wispy beard were gray. On his head, he wore a white cloth hat that angled down around his neck. His plain white robe was held by a tasseled belt of gold braid. Of medium height, he was stout but not flabby. Four grim-faced men in elaborate embroidered robes stood behind him.

"Marco, I did not know you were coming to the palace today. Why did you not have yourself announced to me?"

Polo did not move. "I did not wish to disturb the khan."

"Rise, Marco. Your companions, as well."

Polo straightened; his servants did so just a moment afterward.

Steve and Marcia also stood erect again.

"I am always pleased to see you, Marco," said Kublai Khan. "You have business here today?"

"I seek a new courier working in the palace," said Polo. "My friend, here, is also from Europe and wishes to speak with him."

"Ah." Kublai Khan glanced at Hunter without interest. "Come tomorrow, Marco. We will visit over tea at midday." He walked away, followed by his retainers.

Polo bowed again. The others followed his example once more. When Polo straightened, he grinned at them.

"I am relieved that he is not angry because I failed to announce my presence. I did not expect to see him today."

"Bowing is the acceptable response?" Hunter asked. "What about kneeling and touching one's forehead to the floor? I heard this was the proper posture in the presence of the khan."

"That is true if we are summoned to the throne room for a formal appearance" Polo said. "Here on the palace grounds, that is much too impractical."

"I see."

Marcia nudged Steve's arm and whispered in Chinese, pointing surreptitiously. "That first guy Marco spoke to is coming through the crowd with somebody. Is that MC 5?"

Steve looked through the crowd. He recognized MC 5, whose appearance was identical to that of the other component robots. MC 5 had somehow acquired a plain black robe and black cloth shoes.

"Hunter," he said quietly.

"I see him," Hunter said, also in Chinese. "Remember, he does not know we are from his time or that we have come for him. We must not reveal ourselves before we can apprehend him, or he will flee."

"What are we going to do, then?" Marcia asked. "We have too many witnesses here just to pounce and disappear with him—unless we want to wind up as a vanishing wonder in Polo's memoirs!"

"And we don't have Jane," said Steve.

Hunter switched back to Italian. "I must speak to this man alone, outside the palace walls. I hesitate to ask you for another favor, but can this be arranged?"

"I believe I may be able to help," said Polo. "I will have to speak to—"

Suddenly Steve glimpsed Jane through a crowd of people pursuing their daily business. "Hunter," he interrupted quickly, in Chinese. "Look." He jumped up and pointed through the crowd. Now he could see Wayne and Ishihara, too.

"Be cautious," said Hunter. "We must get MC 5 away from witnesses and we cannot appear to be kidnapping him. Our other disappearance in front of local people during other missions occurred during and prior to battles, among people distracted by immediate, life-threatening situations. We cannot avoid being noticed here."

"But we have to save Jane," said Marcia, standing up next to Steve. "What are we going to do?"

"Vanishing from court could alter the beliefs and expectations regarding religion and court policy, maybe even influence the khan himself," said Hunter. "I cannot take that risk."

Jane spotted Hunter sitting in the shade in a small garden at a distance, between a European man and Steve. Even through the crowd of people walking through the palace grounds between them, Hunter was too big and distinctive to miss. Wayne and Ishihara, on each side of her, had not seemed to see Hunter. However, she could not decide what to do.

A few moments before, Ishihara had spotted MC 5. Now he and Wayne were walking quickly to catch him. MC 5, wearing black, approached Hunter, Steve, and Marcia in the company of a young man. She could see that Hunter must have arranged to have MC 5 brought to him, and she did not want to do anything that would interfere.

"Be ready," Ishihara said. "We cannot just grab him and try to run out of the palace grounds. We must apprehend him together and then instantly trigger the belt unit."

In another few moments of fast walking, however, Jane saw that Ishihara had almost come with an arm's reach of MC 5.

"Hold onto Jane," Wayne ordered.

Ishihara took Jane's wrist.

"Hunter!" Jane screamed as loud as she could.

Hunter, Steve, and Marcia suddenly ran forward

toward MC 5. At the same moment, Ishihara pulled Jane toward the component robot, with Wayne next to her. Jane braced her feet against the paving stones under her, and bent her knees, pulling against Ishihara. Her feet merely skidded on the stones; she did not slow him down noticeably.

Steve ran toward MC 5, but he could see that Ishihara nearly had a hand on the component robot already. Suddenly, however, MC 5 saw Steve, Marcia, and Hunter charging toward him. He first shoved his human companion, the other courier, out of the way; then MC 5 darted in the other direction. Even Ishihara, reaching out with one hand, failed to grab him.

"Hunter, you get MC 5!" Steve shouted as he threw himself on Ishihara.

"Get him!" Jane called, pulling back harder on Ishihara's other arm.

Steve collided bodily with Ishihara and clung to him. "Stop! I order you to stop moving. Let go of Jane."

Ishihara neither released Jane's wrist nor spoke. He grabbed the firmly-tied sash of Steve's robe with his free hand and pulled. Steve lost his grip, stumbled, and fell to the ground. He understood that some First Law imperative had overrode his instructions to Ishihara.

Steve glanced over at Hunter. MC 5 had turned to flee, but Hunter snatched him up off the ground and held him high, kicking and flailing. Steve scrambled to his feet.

"Stop struggling," Steve ordered MC 5 in English. "Keep quiet and don't try to get away."

The small robot obeyed. Hunter set him on his feet again, but held one arm firmly in his grasp. He turned toward Jane.

Wayne had halted in front of Hunter, seeing that he was too late to get MC 5. Ishihara still held Jane's wrist tightly as she struggled against him. Marcia had stopped, uncertain what she should do.

"Steve!" Jane pleaded.

Suddenly Steve leaped forward, this time aiming at Ishihara's outstretched arm as Jane pulled away from him again. Before Steve made contact, however, he saw Ishihara, Jane, and Wayne vanish. He landed hard on the paving stones.

Polo strode up quickly, speaking Italian in a low, urgent tone. "What happened here? Where did they go? What . . . happened?"

Steve looked up, glad he supposedly could not understand Italian.

Hunter and Marcia said nothing.

A small crowd of people had surrounded them, gasping and murmuring.

Polo glanced quickly back over his shoulder. "I do not know what this is about, but the khan saw this incident. He is coming this way. Be very careful how you speak to him."

Quickly, Steve got to his feet. Marcia moved close to him. Hunter, still holding MC 5 in his arms off the ground, turned to look. Kublai Khan and his small entourage hurried up in front of them.

Steve bowed low from the waist again. Since the khan did not bid them to rise, or say anything else right away, he remained in that position. So did Polo and Marcia. Hunter, as he held MC 5's arm, also bowed and held the position, as did MC 5.

All Steve could see were the paving stones below him and the khan's feet, in leather boots that curled up at the toe. For a long moment, no one spoke or moved.

Suddenly Steve wondered if they would all lose their heads.

"What is this magic?" The khan finally demanded in Mongol. "Marco, who were those foreigners who disappeared? Who has cast spells here in my presence?"

Steve thought he could detect an element of fear in the khan's voice, but if so, it was very subtle.

"I do not know," said Polo.

"Rise, all of you. I want to see your faces."

Steve straightened, his heart pounding. Before, all the jumps in time had either taken place away from local people, or else had happened in the middle of chaotic situations where other people's attention had been diverted. If any situation could change history, though, he suspected that having Marco Polo and Kublai Khan witness a disappearance into time might do it.

Kublai Khan looked up into Hunter's eyes. "Stranger, explain this."

Hunter said nothing.

Startled, Steve looked at him in amazement. Always before, Hunter had offered an effective response to any difficult situation. Steve realized that for Hunter, refusing to answer meant that he could not think of anything to say that he considered safe under the Three Laws of Robotics.

Polo nudged Hunter with his elbow.

"I have no explanation," said Hunter in Mongol.

The khan glared at him, then turned to Steve. "Speak."

Steve swallowed. He had no idea what to say, either. "I, uh . . ."

"May I speak?" Marcia spoke softly.

"Speak," said Kublai Khan, turning to her with a piercing gaze.

"We seek evil spirits that tried to infiltrate the great khan's court."

"Eh? Evil spirits?"

Marcia nodded.

"Marco, what do you know of this?"

"Nothing," said Polo. "But I was told this small fellow in Hunter's grasp would do anything to protect you."

"Why are you holding him like this?" The khan asked Hunter.

"He is a good spirit who has lost his way," Marcia said quickly. "He would never let harm come to his khan, but we must return him to his home."

"You bring spirits and magic within my walls without telling me?" Kublai Khan glared at each of them in turn.

"We feared the khan would not believe our story," said Steve.

"That is correct," said Hunter. "We had hoped to handle this matter without disturbing the khan."

"I have just seen three people disappear with my own eyes," said Kublai Khan. "Until now, I would not have believed this."

"We are dealing with good spirits," said Marcia. "But I suggest that neither Marco nor the khan speak of this."

"No?" Kublai Khan studied her carefully.

"What about everybody else?" Steve asked her quietly.

"I don't believe the others will matter."

"Marco, what is your opinion of this?" Kublai Khan turned to him.

"I have seen many wonders since I entered the khan's empire," said Marco. "Many would not be believed back in Venice. This is another one of those."

"I will not have anyone think I have gone mad," said Kublai Khan. "However, that includes your friends." He turned to Marcia again. "Why should I believe you? How do I know this is not some elaborate game, conducted to make a fool of me?"

"We can prove our claim to your satisfaction." She glanced at Hunter. "We can do what those spirits did."

Hunter nodded acknowledgment. Still holding MC 5's arm, he slipped his other hand inside his robe. He waited, watching Marcia.

Steve got the idea. "If we prove to Marco and the khan that we are dealing in spirits and possess magic, will the khan accept our advice not to discuss this matter or act on it in the future?"

"If you confer with good spirits and prove your magic, I will accept your advice," said Kublai Khan.

"So will I," said Polo.

"Okay, Hunter?" Steve grinned at him.

"We must step away from them," said Hunter. He backed away from Polo, drawing MC 5 with him.

Steve and Marcia moved to his side.

Polo turned. Standing only a step away from the khan and his entourage, he looked at Hunter with a puzzled expression. None of them spoke.

"Good-bye, Marco Polo," Marcia said softly in Mongol. "Farewell, Great Khan. I was honored to meet both of you."

As Polo glanced toward her, the scene vanished.

Once again, Steve felt the hard, curved interior surface of the sphere in Room F-12 under him. He and Marcia slid against each other in the blackness. Then Hunter opened the sphere and helped them both climb out.

"Get out," Steve said to MC 5. "Don't shut off your hearing or go anywhere."

R. Daladier still stood by the door. "Dr. Nystrom and Ishihara have not been back here."

Hunter nodded. "Thank you. Please continue your assignment here until further notice."

"Agreed."

"It feels weird not to have Jane with us," said Steve. "And what about disappearing in front of Marco Polo and Kublai Khan? What if we did change history this time?"

"We will not know for a while yet," said Hunter. "I can see that the sphere and this room are unchanged."

"That's something, anyway." Steve nodded. "I'm ready to go find Jane anytime."

"You still need a good night's rest before our next mission," said Hunter.

"I feel okay." Steve shrugged.

"In any case, I will have to prepare more vaccinations and hire a new historian," said Hunter. "For now, you and Marcia should change your clothes."

"I'll go first," said Marcia. She picked up her regular clothes and went into the other room.

"I am concerned about Jane, also," said Hunter. "However, I trust we will all meet again on our next mission to find MC 6. We will prepare for it in the same way as the others. I will make the arrangements and you will have some time to rest, eat well, and relax."

"I won't relax too well this time," said Steve. "But I'll be ready."

By the time Steve had taken his turn to change, Hunter had arranged for a Security vehicle to take the team and MC 5 back to MC Governor's office. Steve instructed MC 5 to come with them, and they rode through the quiet streets of Mojave Center. No one spoke. From past experience, Steve knew that Hunter was monitoring news reports to make sure that no explosion had destroyed Beijing and find out if and where another nuclear explosion had occurred.

In Mojave Center Governor's office, Hunter closed the door and turned to Steve.

"Please instruct MC 5 to merge with the others."

Steve pointed to the figure standing in the corner. The first four component robots stood merged there. "Join with them," he said to MC 5. "Then remain motionless here, just like the other component robots now are."

The small robot walked over to them. In a slow, slithering motion, his shape became fluid and he merged with the other figure. Now it nearly resembled the large, humanoid shape of Mojave Center Governor.

"We are doing well," said Hunter. "We have only one more piece of the puzzle to find."

"You must have checked the news by now," said Steve. "Did we *really* get away with vanishing in front of Marco Polo and Kublai Khan?"

"In my monitoring of the news, I have not detected any sign of change in our world," said Hunter. "And Mojave Center appears to be the same as before. That is only a superficial review, of course. I am also accessing historical references in the city library as we speak. So far, they confirm my initial conclusion."

"I think we got away with it," said Marcia. "I thought this through before I started talking to Kublai Khan, but I didn't have any way to explain it to you."

"What do you mean?" Steve asked.

"As I mentioned before we left, Marco Polo said on his deathbed that in his book, he had not told half the wonders he had seen on his travels. I think he also omitted witnessing spirits who vanished before his eyes."

"But what about Kublai Khan and all those other people standing around us?" Steve frowned. "I was glad to get out of there, but wouldn't at least a few of them change their beliefs about the world or religion?"

"That's the other part I had to consider," said Marcia. "But most of the people there—maybe all of them—believed in some form of Chinese or Mongol animistic religion. Even the Buddhists and Taoists in China had open attitudes toward folk deities and spirits. Kublai Khan himself instituted state tolerance of all religions and seemed to consider them equally valid. I don't think we altered anyone's beliefs because they *already* believed that spirits in human form came and went around them."

"Kublai Khan said he didn't want anyone to think he was crazy," said Steve.

"If the great khan did not want the incident mentioned again, I can guarantee that no one in the palace grounds spoke of it openly," said Marcia. "A few whispers in private or some rumors outside the walls in the city after hours would simply get lost among other unprovable reports of spirit visitations."

"Your explanation seems sound," said Hunter.

"What about MC 6?" Steve asked.

"The news headlines report a nuclear explosion in southern England near the Welsh border," Hunter said grimly. "Like the others, it has killed millions of people."

"Did you get the date we're going to visit from the sphere console?" Steve asked.

"Yes. MC 6 will return to his full size in A.D. 460. At that time, a man named Arturius, upon whom the legend of King Arthur was based, was the most powerful individual in Britain."

AVONOVA PRESENTS
AWARD-WINNING NOVELS
FROM MASTERS OF SCIENCE FICTION

WULFSYARN
by Phillip Mann   71717-4/ $4.99 US

MIRROR TO THE SKY
by Mark S. Geston   71703-4/ $4.99 US/ $5.99 Can

THE DESTINY MAKERS
by George Turner   71887-1/ $4.99 US/ $5.99 Can

A DEEPER SEA
by Alexander Jablokov   71709-3/ $4.99 US/ $5.99 Can

BEGGARS IN SPAIN
by Nancy Kress   71877-4/ $4.99 US/ $5.99 Can

FLYING TO VALHALLA
by Charles Pellegrino   71881-2/ $4.99 US/ $5.99 Can

ETERNAL LIGHT
by Paul J. McAuley   76623-X/ $4.99 US/ $5.99 Can